CHRISTMAS CAROLS AT ROOKERY HOUSE

ROSIE HENDRY

Christmas Carols at Rookery House

Copyright © 2024 by Rosie Hendry
ISBN: 978-1-914443-34-3

Published by Rookery House Press
Cover design by designforwriters.com

For David,
with love and thanks.

CHAPTER 1

Early December 1942 – Lancaster

Flo Butterworth stared at the view she'd seen countless times before, a feeling of home settling comfortingly inside her. This place, her grandad's allotment, had inspired and helped nurture her love of growing things from as far back as she could remember. It had also become a place of refuge for her after her parents, sister and brother had been killed, almost two years ago now, in the Manchester Christmas Blitz, when Flo had fled to Lancaster to be with her remaining family.

'A penny for them?' Her grandad's voice broke into her thoughts, his Lancashire accent so familiar and reassuring along with the sweet smell of the tobacco smoke spiralling up from his pipe into the chilly air.

Flo glanced at him sitting next to her on the bench outside his shed, looking over the frost-dusted allotment he'd tended so lovingly for as long as she could remember.

'I was just thinking about how this place makes me feel.

What it's given me.' She gestured with her hand towards the neat rows of winter vegetables, which even at this time of year provided plenty of food for her grandparents and a welcome addition to their rations. 'And how much I've learned by working with you here.'

'I remember you helping me right from when you were a nipper,' he said fondly. 'You always enjoyed getting your hands in the soil, planting and sowing seeds.' He chuckled. 'And you still do! Places like this are important in other ways too.' He puffed on his pipe. 'They give you a chance to mull things over, a place to be quiet and focus on the plants. It gives your mind a rest from problems and sometimes even helps you find the answer while you're otherwise occupied.'

Flo nodded in agreement. 'I don't know where I'd be now, or what I would be doing, if I hadn't had this place and then our family allotments to learn from. I'd probably never have even thought about becoming a Land Girl.' Her eyes drifted over to the far side of the allotments where her parents had once had a plot before they'd all upped-sticks and moved to Manchester for her father's job back in 1936. She'd spent so many happy hours working there alongside her mam, dad, sister and brother but now it was another family's.

Her grandad took the pipe out of his mouth and looked at her, a concerned expression on his face. 'You're still enjoying your Land Girl work, aren't you?'

'I am, and I love what I do, along with living at Rookery House and the good friends I've made in Norfolk. I couldn't have asked for anymore, only that...' Flo fell silent. Her wish that the bomb had never fallen on her family home, killing her parents, sister Joyce and brother Bobby, didn't need voicing. It was something she'd wished thousands of times before and no doubt would thousands more until her dying day. But there was absolutely nothing she could do to change what had happened and how it had catapulted her life off in an unexpected direction.

Her grandad patted her hand briefly as he puffed on his pipe again. 'We all wish that one day had never happened to us, and for the war to have left our family well alone.'

They fell into silence for a few minutes, Flo's thoughts going back to that night on 22nd December almost two years ago, her heart aching at the memory. She had been in the kitchen washing up after making a large batch of mince pies using the precious jar of mincemeat that her mother had saved especially. With rationing the way it was, it was unlikely they'd have been able to buy another jar for some time, so those pies were to be treasured and savoured.

Flo recalled how the kitchen had been fragrant with the scent of spices and rich dried fruits as the pies cooled on the rack. She'd been happy at the prospect of the coming Christmas and was looking forward to a few days off work, spending them at home with her family. She had been singing as she worked, enjoying the words and music of her favourite carol, *The Holly and the Ivy*, when Joyce had come into the kitchen to top up the hot water bottles for their mam and brother who were both in bed poorly with the flu. Flo was desperately hoping they'd be well enough to get up for Christmas Day.

She remembered her dad coming indoors wearing his blue ARP overalls, ready to go out on duty. He'd wanted a mince pie, tempted by the smell, but Flo had refused to let him have one, telling him they had to be saved for Christmas. Oh, how many times since had she wished she'd said yes to him! Let him enjoy some. It had been shortly after that when the air-raid siren had sounded and her dad had sent her outside to prepare the Anderson down at the bottom of the garden, while he and Joyce helped Mam and Bobby downstairs. Only they'd never got to the shelter. Not even one of them. A bomb had fallen on the neighbour's adjoining house, the explosion blasting through into their home, causing it to crumple, trapping and killing her family in the rubble.

Flo blinked at the tears stinging her eyes, her throat painful. She tried hard these days not to go back to that night, not to relive the details, wishing over and over that it hadn't happened. Wondering if only she'd done something differently, might her family have survived, if not all, then at least some of them? Of course, she couldn't turn back the clock and, after talking to people about what had happened, she knew logically that it was pure chance that the bomb landed where it did. There was nothing she could have done to change it or stop it. If it had been her sister who'd been sent out to organise the shelter rather than her, then Flo would have probably been killed instead.

A tear ran down her cheek and she wiped it away with the back of her hand.

'I know, lass. I know.' Her grandad's voice was gruff. He puffed on his pipe for a moment, the embers in the bowl glowing orange, then he said, 'Tell me more about this WI allotment you help with.'

Flo turned to him, appreciating his kind attempt to distract her.

'Have I told you about Percy Blake and how he ended up having to buy lettuces from the WI stall at the summer fete because all his were eaten by slugs? It pleased the WI members no end. Percy and his pals had been rather too dismissive of our ladies when they first got their plot,' Flo said, glad to change the subject.

Both her grandparents took a keen interest in Flo and her work as a Land Girl in Great Plumstead and her weekly letters to them were full of what she did and saw there. Since she'd come to visit them, they'd had many discussions about Rookery House and the friends Flo had made, as well as the things she was involved with in the village like the WI allotment and the singing group. It was important to Flo that they knew about her life and remained connected, no matter how far from her they were for most of the year. The letters between Flo and her grandparents were precious, and even more so was this holiday. After being with them here in Lancaster for a week, it was almost time for her to return to Rookery House. Flo decided she would not waste a second more of it feeling sad.

'What jobs can I do for you today?' Flo asked, getting to her feet and giving her grandad a warm smile. 'Put me to work while I'm here.'

He laughed. 'I've got just the job for you. You can help me give the greenhouse a good clear-out and wash the plant pots ready for spring sowing.'

'If we're lucky, the sun will come out and heat up the greenhouse for us while we're in there.' Flo looked up at the sky where patches of blue were appearing as the grey clouds were blown eastwards by a fresh December wind coming in from the Irish Sea. 'So come on,' she held out her hand for her grandad to take as he got to his feet, 'let's get to work!'

CHAPTER 2

Great Plumstead Hall Hospital — Norfolk

'The ambulance is nearly here! It's coming down the drive,' Evie's friend and fellow VAD nurse Hazel Robertson announced as she hurried into Dining Room Ward.

Evie was doing a final check to make sure everything was ready to receive their new intake of patients after they'd spent the morning preparing for their arrival.

'Are we all set?' Hazel asked, looking about her.

'Yes, as far as I can see.' Evie gave Hazel a reassuring smile and lowered her voice to add, 'It's exactly as Matron would expect.'

Earlier, they'd waved off four men who'd been convalescing here at the Red Cross Military Hospital in Great Plumstead Hall and who were now sufficiently recovered to be discharged from their care. Evie found saying goodbye to her patients a bittersweet experience. On the one hand, it was gratifying that the nursing they'd received here had helped the patients recover enough to leave, but the fact that some of them would be returning to fight again was hard to accept. There was always the risk that the men might not be so lucky the next time they encountered the enemy. They could lose their life instead of sustaining recoverable injuries.

Of this morning's four discharged patients, two were going home for good, as they were now considered unfit for active service, but the other men would be heading back to their units after a period of leave. As always, Evie had wished them all well and added silently that those returning to battle would stay safe and make it through unscathed to the end of the war.

'Come on then, let's go and welcome our new patients.' Hazel grabbed hold of Evie's arm and led her out into the wide hallway with its black and white tiled floor and grand staircase leading to the upper storeys.

As they went out through the front door, Evie was pleased to see that it was a WVS ambulance bringing today's patients with her friend Thea Thornton at the wheel. Evie was one of Thea's lodgers who lived with her at Rookery House in the village. Evie waved as Thea steered the ambulance around in a circle and brought it to a halt by the door. Thea and her WVS colleague Pat often transported patients here to convalesce after their initial surgery or treatment at the larger Norfolk and Norwich Hospital in the city.

'Good morning,' Thea greeted them as she climbed out of the ambulance cab, dressed in a pair of green WVS overalls and overcoat, with a matching green beret on her curly, brown, bob-length hair. 'We've got four patients for you. Is that how many you're expecting?'

'That's right,' Evie said, walking around to the ambulance's back doors with Thea and Pat. 'Everything's ready for them.'

Thea nodded. 'I'm sure they'll be glad to get indoors in the warm.' Her breath clouded in the chilly air as she spoke.

'We've wrapped them up well with blankets and hot water bottles, but it's cold out today and lying still on a stretcher doesn't generate much body heat.'

'Let's get them in as quick as we can.' Evie knew that the next hour was going to be busy settling the men in and giving them a chance to recover from the journey.

Thea opened the back doors and, with the ease of plenty of practice, she and Pat slid the first stretcher out of its rungs. Evie noticed the raised blankets draped over a cage protecting the patient's lower legs and the shape of only one foot at the bottom of the stretcher – this man had lost a limb.

'Welcome to Great Plumstead Hall Hospital!' Evie gave him a welcoming smile. 'We'll soon have you settled in and warmed up.'

'Thank you,' he said gratefully.

Thea and Pat carried him in through the front door, which Hazel opened to admit them, and Evie followed on. She was about to tell them which empty bed to take the new patient to in Dining Room Ward but was cut off by the arrival of Matron Reed, who swept across the hallway from the direction of her office like a ship in full sail.

'Who have we here?' Matron asked in her soft Scottish voice, holding up her hand to halt Thea and Pat. She took the patient's notes out from where they were tucked into a blanket near his remaining foot and, after a quick scan of them, said, 'Welcome, Flight Sergeant Parish, we'll get you into your bed in just a moment. Ladies, if you can take our patient to the right and nearest the fireplace, please. And Nurse Jones...' she focused her steely gaze on Evie, 'don't just stand there doing nothing, get the bedding turned down ready to transfer Flight Sergeant Parish into his bed.'

Evie ignored the annoyance that flared inside her at Matron's unnecessary rebuke and hurried into the ward to do as she was told. It was always the same when a new intake arrived. Matron became irritated and snapped at the nurses, no matter how competent they were and how many times they'd successfully welcomed and settled in new patients before. If Matron hadn't appeared when she had, Evie and Hazel would have been more than capable of organising the beds appropriately for the new men. To survive working under the rule of Matron Reed, Evie'd had to develop a thick skin to deflect the older woman's sharp comments – well most of them, she thought wryly as she pulled the neatly tucked-in crisp white sheet and blue blankets from one edge of the bed so that Flight Sergeant Parish could be made comfortable without a moment's delay.

'On the count of three,' Thea said after she and Pat had rested the stretcher on the side of the bed and removed the blankets, cage and hot water bottle surrounding their charge. 'One, two, three…'

With Evie's help, they eased the young man into his bed, ever mindful of his injuries. After replacing the cage over his leg, which had been amputated below the knee, Evie put hospital hot water bottles either side of him and then quickly tucked him in.

'You'll soon warm up in there and I'll get you a cup of tea in a minute or two, which will help as well,' Evie told him.

'A cup of tea sounds smashing, thank you,' Flight Sergeant Parish said in his Yorkshire accent, his cheeks looking rosy after coming in from outside. 'And thanks for the ride here,' he said to Thea and Pat.

'You're welcome.' Thea touched his shoulder. 'You rest up and recover. You'll be well looked after here.'

After Thea and Pat had gone to fetch another patient from the ambulance, Flight Sergeant Parish looked around the room, his brown eyes registering surprise at the ornate ceiling with its fancy design. 'It's much grander in here than what we've been used to at the Norfolk and Norwich Hospital.'

'I'm sure it is,' Evie agreed, checking his covers were well tucked in, knowing Matron would pick up on it if they weren't. 'The family who owns the house ate their meals in here – and held grand dinner parties too, I expect. But for now it's being put to another more important use, I think.'

Once all the new patients were safely in their beds, Evie headed off to the kitchen to fetch tea and biscuits for them. As always, receiving a new intake of men brought with it a period of readjustment. The nurses had to get to know their patients with their differing personalities and nursing requirements. Although two of the new patients were bed-bound, the other two were mobile, one on crutches and the other convalescing after surgery for appendicitis. The variety of individual needs kept things fresh and interesting, Evie thought as she made her way along the corridor in the old servants' quarters towards the kitchen. She'd grown to enjoy every aspect of her nursing work and had learned so much from her patients as they talked about their life and experiences.

Best of all, she'd met Ned Blythe, who'd been a patient recovering from an injury to his eyes. She'd known Ned vaguely in her old life, when he had worked as a chauffeur for her parents-in-law before the war. She and Ned had developed a wonderful friendship during his stay at the hospital, and after he'd been medically discharged from the army, the two of them had kept in touch by letter. To her surprise, Ned returned to take up a job working as a gardener here at the hall. Slowly their friendship deepened, and they'd been stepping out together for almost a whole year. After Evie's disastrous and abusive marriage, another relationship was something she had never expected or even wanted. It was Ned's kindness, gentleness and caring ways that had overcome her reservations and made her take a chance with him, and it had worked. Now that she had Ned in her life she was happy, and she hoped nothing would ever spoil it.

CHAPTER 3

Rookery House, Great Plumstead

Thea had a willing assistant on this bright, but chilly, winter morning. It was Saturday and just as he did each weekend, or during the school holidays, seven-year-old George was helping her look after the animals at Rookery House. He'd already taken Primrose out to the meadow after she'd been milked, the gentle Jersey cow allowing him to lead her by her halter, and then he'd fed the rabbits. Now, Thea and George were in the orchard collecting eggs from the nest boxes of the wooden chicken coop.

'Why don't chickens lay so many in winter?' George asked, picking up one of the brown speckled eggs from the straw-lined nest box and placing it carefully in the wicker basket.

'Because the days are shorter, so there's less light. And because several of the hens have just moulted and lost some of their feathers. Now they must put their energy into growing new ones instead of laying,' Thea explained. 'But we're lucky to still have a lot more eggs to eat than most people are allowed on their rations.'

George looked up at her, his face serious beneath the blue woolly hat Hettie had knitted for him. 'The chickens will lay more eggs again in the spring, won't they?'

'Yes. Everything does better in the springtime. Longer days and warmer weather help the plants to grow, too. Nature wakes up and makes the most of it.'

'And the bees will come out again.' George pointed towards the beehives that stood at the far end of the orchard.

'They will, and they'll be ready to pollinate the blossom on our apple, plum and pear trees. We'll all look forward to spring after the cold winter days.' Thea gave one last glance around the nest box to make sure they'd gathered all the eggs, then closed and fastened the lid. 'Shall we go for a walk around Five Acres after we've taken these back to the house?'

George nodded and slipped his gloved hand into Thea's.

The path around the perimeter of Five Acres field was a route the pair of them often took on their walks. In the springtime they peeped in the hedgerows looking for birds' nests, where they'd marvel at the intricately constructed nests and the delicately patterned eggs inside. Many boys enjoyed collecting wild birds' eggs, but not George. He wanted each one to hatch and for every chick to have a chance of fledging out into the world. Once they found a nest, he always kept a close eye on the chicks and their parents, minding what Thea had taught him – not to interfere with them, but to observe the goings-on from a safe distance. Now, with the hedgerow bare of leaves, the once hidden empty nests stood out amongst the twigs and branches.

'Look at this.' Thea reached into the thorny thicket of a

blackthorn hedge and took out a beautiful oval-shaped nest constructed from moss, lichen and fine spiders' silk.

George touched the nest with the tip of his finger, running it over the surface, which was a stunning combination of sea-green grey, greeny blues and mustard yellow, coloured by the natural materials from which it was made.

'Here, you hold it.' Thea put the nest into George's cupped hands and watched as the little boy's face lit up. 'Feel how light it is.'

'It's like there's hardly anything there!' he said.

'Have a peep inside,' Thea encouraged him, gently parting the entrance hole of the nest so they could both see.

'It's so different!' George poked his little finger in and stroked the feather lining. 'So soft and warm for the chicks. We'd better put it back ready for the spring.' He carefully handed Thea the nest and she returned it to where she'd found it.

'We'll keep an eye on it and see if the long-tailed tits use it again,' Thea said.

Carrying on with their walk, they stopped frequently to look at things. They were watching a spider lurking at the entrance of its tunnel-like web spun in a gorse bush when the noise of engines overhead made them look up. One of the planes from RAF Great Plumstead was circling round before going into land and then immediately taking off again.

'They must be practising their circuits and bumps,' Thea said. 'Elspeth told me that's what the pilots call it.' Thea had become more knowledgeable about the activities at the aerodrome, and the RAF lingo, since getting to know Elspeth and Marge, the two Waafs who'd come to stay with them for a few weeks earlier in the year.

'Would you like to fly, Auntie Thea?' George asked.

'In a plane, you mean?'

14

'No. Fly like a bird. Just flap your arms and take off.' He demonstrated by flapping his arms vigorously. 'I would fly up into the sky.' George's face had an eager look. 'I'd love to do that.'

'It would be a marvellous thing to do, indeed.' Thea put her arm around the little boy's shoulders. 'But unfortunately for us humans, the only way we can fly is inside an aeroplane or a hot-air balloon.'

George looked up at her. 'Would you fly in an aeroplane if you could?'

She considered for a moment. 'I think so. It would be amazing to be up there and see what the birds can see. Would you?'

George quickly nodded. 'Do you think they might let me have a ride in one of the planes at the aerodrome?' His voice was hopeful.

'Probably not,' Thea said gently. 'They're too busy flying missions to just take people up for a ride. But maybe one day you'll be able to fly in an aeroplane, when you're older.' They walked on a little further. 'I was thinking we must write to your mum this afternoon. Ask her if she'd like to come and spend Christmas with us.'

'I hope she'll say yes,' George said. 'Do you think she will?'

'I'm sure she will, if she can,' Thea reassured him.

Jess Collins, George and his sister Betty's mother, had been evacuated out to the village with her children, but after a few months had returned to London again, leaving them here for their safety. It couldn't have been easy for Jess, but she kept in regular contact writing letters and visiting as often as she could. She'd spent a week here in August during the school summer holidays and it would be lovely if she could also come for Christmas at Rookery House this year.

'And Flo will be home soon too,' George said. 'I've missed her a *lot*.'

'It doesn't seem right here without her, does it? We're all looking forward to her coming back today.'

'What time will she be back? Can we go to the station to meet her?'

'She won't be home till late tonight as she's got a long way to come. All the way from Lancaster, so I don't know exactly what time she'll be here,' Thea said. 'You might not see her until tomorrow morning.'

George nodded. 'I'll show her the long-tail tit's nest tomorrow then. I think she'll like it.'

'I'm sure she will,' Thea agreed with a smile. It was a delight to see the close relationship Flo and George had forged. The pair often spent time together outside or playing board games indoors, and Flo took great pleasure reading his beloved books to him. Thea suspected that the little boy reminded Flo of the younger brother she'd lost in the bombing of her family home. Spending time with George helped Flo as much as it did George.

CHAPTER 4

Manchester

Flo stared at the grey granite gravestone marking the last resting place of her family. She still found it hard to believe it was where they were now and that she'd never see them again or hear their voices. Seeing their names written on the simple headstone brought tears to her eyes and she didn't stop them, letting them run unchecked down her cheeks, the chilly wind making them feel as if they were made from ice.

She had broken her long journey back to Rookery House with a stop in Manchester so she could come here to the cemetery in the city, wanting to visit the grave and lay a wreath in memory of her family. Flo had made the wreath from greenery she'd gathered from the hedgerow near her grandad's Lancaster allotment, entwining spiky-leaved holly with lengths of glossy ivy. It was simple, but beautiful. The red holly berries stood out vividly against the dark green foliage. It felt fitting to bring a piece of Lancaster here for them, something from the place where all her family had been born and lived for most of their lives.

Placing the wreath against the gravestone, she stepped back, bowing her head.

'I wish you were still here,' she said softly. 'I miss you all so much. Every single day.'

But there was no reply, just the sound of the wind blowing through the leafless branches of the tall trees surrounding the cemetery. Flo lingered on, reluctant to leave. Her visits to the grave were few and far between as she was only able to come when she had leave and was either on her way to, or back from, seeing her grandparents. It pained her that for most of the time the grave lay bare with no flowers to show that someone cared and remembered those who'd died, because she did. So very much. But then a bunch of flowers was only a token, Flo reminded herself, and they would soon fade and shrivel. The important thing was that she would always carry her parents, sister and brother in her heart – and that was with her wherever she went.

Laying her hand on the top of the gravestone, she paused for a moment before saying, 'I'll be back again as soon as I can.' Then Flo picked up her suitcase and, with a last glance at the grave, left to make her way to the station and continue her long journey back to Rookery House.

CHAPTER 5

Great Plumstead Hall Hospital

It was Monday morning and Evie was putting away the recent delivery of clean laundry. She carefully checked each item on the list to ensure they'd received the same number of sheets and pillowcases back that had been sent out to wash. Matron was most particular about making sure nothing went astray.

This was a job Evie always enjoyed doing as it was a quiet contrast from the hustle and bustle of the wards or the Recreation Room. Here it was peaceful and gave her a chance to catch her breath for a little while as she put the smoothly pressed linen away, with its clean, lingering scent of soap. Stepping back, she checked that the edges of each folded sheet were aligned in a neat pile in the cupboards of what had once been the Butler's pantry, unaware someone had joined her in the room and was watching her. When a familiar Scottish voice spoke, it startled her, and she felt her heart pick up its pace.

'Was everything returned correctly?' Matron strode across the room from where she'd been standing just inside the doorway and picked up the list on which Evie had ticked off each item as she'd checked it. Matron's eyes scanned down the list slowly, checking for herself. 'Yes, it's exactly as it should be.' She handed Evie the list.

Evie took it and closed the glass-fronted door of the cupboard, her pulse returning to normal. Coming into rooms and catching nurses unawares with her soft footsteps was a habit of Matron's and one she no doubt used deliberately to keep her staff on their toes. For a woman of stout build, she could be remarkably light and swift of foot when needed.

Matron glanced at the watch pinned to the front of her uniform. 'It's half past twelve now. You've time to take a message to Mr White in the bothy for me before we have our meal at one o'clock.'

Evie smiled inwardly at the prospect of going out to where Ned would likely be having his break. Despite them both working at the Hall they didn't always see each other every day so the chance to run into him delighted her.

'Lady Campbell-Gryce is putting me in charge of decorating the hallway this year, with the help of nursing staff and patients who're able and willing,' Matron Reed continued. 'She's arranged for a Christmas tree to be carried in from the estate on the morning of the twenty-second. Boxes of decorations will be brought down from the attic. How we decorate is entirely up to me and I'd like plenty of greenery – holly, ivy, pine – that sort of thing, and some Christmas roses if possible. Can you place an order with Mr White to deliver them to the hallway by ten o'clock on the twenty-second? Make it clear to him that I expect there to be plenty of *red berries* on the holly.'

'Yes Matron,' Evie said, eager to be on her way.

'And I suppose we'd better add some sprigs of mistletoe to that order too, do you think?' The older woman raised an eyebrow, her shrewd brown eyes regarding Evie.

Feeling her cheeks grow warm, Evie recalled how Matron had caught her and Ned kissing under the mistletoe last Christmas Day while the hall was filled with couples dancing around them, Matron included, with Mr White as her dance partner. If Evie wasn't mistaken, there was a hint of a smile playing at the corners of Matron's mouth.

'Of course, Matron,' Evie replied, keeping her voice neutral, 'I will tell Mr White.'

'Good. Now get along, and I will expect you back ready to eat at one o'clock sharp.' Matron turned on her well-polished heels and strode out of the room.

With no time to waste, Evie added the checked laundry list to the pile of others in a drawer and headed for the staff cloakroom to put on her coat before going out to the garden.

Outside there was an icy wind blowing and it needled its way between gaps in her heavy greatcoat and blue wool scarf. She put a gloved hand on her head to stop her nurse's white veil from being blown off as she headed to the bothy. The veil was such a nuisance to put on each morning with its exacting pleats and so many hairpins securing it in place in her auburn hair. Evie didn't want it to come undone as she'd have to redo it again before her meal at one o'clock.

'Hello Evie!' a voice called out to her as she opened the arched wooden door in the perimeter wall of the vegetable garden and stepped through it.

'Hello!' She greeted Prue, who was Thea's sister and a frequent visitor to Rookery House. Prue was dressed in her green WVS uniform and was pushing the pram she used to transport pies for the village's Rural Pie Scheme. She strode towards Evie along a path between the vegetable beds.

'Have you sold out for today?' Evie asked. She had forgotten it was the weekly pie delivery; Ned and Mr White would now be tucking into the pies they'd ordered the week before.

'I have. They're all gone.' Prue gestured towards the two empty baskets that were tucked inside the pram where a baby would normally lay. 'This was my last stop for today but if you want me to bring you a pie next week, you can order one from me now.'

'I'd love to, but I don't think it would go down well with Matron. All of us nurses have our meals with her in the staff sitting room and there's even a hierarchy of who sits where. She wouldn't approve of me eating a pie out in the bothy instead.'

'Fair enough. We don't want to upset Matron.' Prue gave her an understanding smile. 'But if you're quick, Ned might still have some of his pie left, so you could take a bite from it!'

Evie let out a laugh. 'I'd best get along quickly then – good to see you!'

'And you,' Prue called as Evie hurried off to the far side of the kitchen garden.

Reaching the bothy, which was built against the perimeter wall, Evie knocked on the wooden door and then let herself in, glad to step out of the icy wind. Immediately her senses were hit by two things: the warmth from the stove and the delicious aroma of pies. Evie's stomach gave an appreciative rumble as it was a long time since breakfast.

'Evie!' Ned stood up from the high stool he was sitting on at one side of the stove, his face breaking into a wide, welcoming smile. 'What are you doing here?'

'Hello,' she returned his smile. 'I've come with a request from Matron for Mr White.' Evie turned her attention to the head gardener, who lounged in his threadbare armchair on the other side of the stove, a half-eaten pie in his hands.

'Oh aye, what does she want now?' Mr White gestured for Evie to take Ned's seat opposite him.

'I'm sorry to disturb your meal but Matron has an order for some Christmas greenery.' Evie explained in more detail what was required.

'That shouldn't be a problem,' Mr White said. 'The Christmas roses have got a lot of buds this year, so tell Matron I'll be sure to send her some along with everything else.'

'Thank you.' Evie gave the head gardener a grateful smile. She knew he understood Matron very well and wouldn't have forgotten his experience of her taking the lead and whisking him around the dance floor last Christmas, whether he'd wanted to or not.

'I'll pick some nice-looking greenery,' Ned said. 'We want it looking good for the men stuck in hospital over Christmas.'

'I appreciate that. How are your pies? I passed Prue on the way in.'

'Delicious!' Mr White said through a mouthful of crumbs, a few falling onto the front of his green waistcoat, which he brushed away with his hand.

'Want to try some of mine?' Ned held up what was left of his pie. 'It's a cheese and onion and very tasty.'

'It smells good.' Evie took a bite and closed her eyes as she chewed; the savoury cheese and onion, combined with the pastry, filled her mouth with a burst of flavour. 'It's delicious,' she agreed after swallowing her mouthful.

'Makes a welcome change from sandwiches,' Ned said, offering her another bite.

'Thank you, but you eat it. It's your meal and I've got to get back to the nurses' sitting room to have mine.' She glanced at the clock on the wall and saw it was just after ten minutes to one. 'I must go, or I'll be late. Thank you, Mr White, I will let Matron know what you said and…' she put her hand on Ned's arm, 'thank you for sharing your pie.'

Ned gave a nod of his head. 'You're welcome. I'll show you out.'

Following her through the bothy door, he gave her a kiss and smiled, his eyes tender behind his round glasses. 'It was a lovely surprise to see you.'

'And you. I was delighted when Matron gave me this job so I could come out here and see you but now I really must go. She's very particular about us not being late for mealtimes… along with everything else, as you know. I'll see you soon.' Evie popped another kiss on Ned's lips before hurrying back to the hospital.

CHAPTER 6

'One good thing about spreading compost is that it keeps you warm!' Flo said, taking her brown Land Army coat off despite the chilly wind and hanging it over a nearby wooden fence. Her dark green Land Army pullover and fawn aertex shirt, along with her brown corduroy breeches, were enough while she was working.

It was Monday afternoon and her first day at work after her visit to Lancaster. She'd arrived back at Rookery House late on Saturday night and had a day to recover from the lengthy journey before starting her job again.

'I'm hoping this will work as well as Ted says it does.' Thea dug her spade into the wheelbarrow full of well-rotted compost and then spread the spadeful over the surface of the vegetable bed.

'I told my grandad about what Ted recommended, and how he'd experimented with spreading compost on the top of the soil rather than digging it in when he was a head gardener. Grandad said he's going to give it a go himself. Said if it saves him from back-breaking digging and still grows good vegetables and fruit, then he'll be a happy man!' Flo shovelled another spade full of rich-brown, crumbly compost from the wheelbarrow and added it to the four-inch layer she was piling around the raspberry canes.

Flo had only known Ted Ellison for a few months. She first met him after an unexploded bomb had fallen in Five Acres field here at Rookery House, and he had been part of the village's Home Guard platoon who'd guarded it while they waited for the Bomb Disposal squad to arrive. Since then, Ted had taught her and Thea a lot, sharing his vast knowledge and experience of growing fruit and vegetables.

Flo leaned on her spade for a moment. 'I suppose it makes sense if you think about it. Before humans started ploughing and digging, leaves and animal dung would have just dropped onto the soil and rotted, and the worms would have worked the remains into the earth. It's the natural way. And it saves us from the horrible experience of accidentally chopping worms in half when we're digging over a garden!'

'If this no-digging method works well, it will save us a lengthy job,' Thea agreed, pausing her work for a moment. 'I've learned a lot from Ted, something new every time he comes here.'

'And that seems to be quite often!' Flo grinned. 'I don't think he's really coming to see us, you know. Although he pretends otherwise.'

Thea smiled. 'He certainly seems to have an eye for Hettie, but she won't hear a word of it! And yet I think Ted's growing on her.'

Flo laughed. 'It's lovely. Ted's such a smashing fellow and they make a fine couple.'

'Steady on!' Thea said. 'I don't think they're quite at that stage...'

Flo's eyes met Thea's and she winked. 'Maybe, but I think Ted would like them to be some day soon.'

'We'll see. The main thing is they are both happy. That's what's important in life and I know Hettie won't be rushed into anything she's not certain about.'

'In the meantime, Ted can keep on teaching us the best way to grow things.' Flo shovelled up another spadeful of the compost which had spent months being broken down from waste plants, raked-up leaves and the manure from animal bedding into a rich, fertile mixture. 'Alice would have loved this new method. She didn't enjoy digging.'

'At least she won't have to do any of that now she's in the WAAF,' Thea said, thinking of her niece who had worked in the Rookery House gardens until she signed up to do her bit for the war effort. 'Now Alice is a fully qualified Wireless Operator there's no need for her to do any digging – she'll be happy about that.'

'She's enjoying what she's doing and I'm pleased for her. Though I do miss her,' Flo said. 'But we keep in touch and who knows she might get posted to an aerodrome in Norfolk.'

'That would be nice,' Thea agreed. 'But she could just as well end up in the north of Scotland. In a way, it would be better for her to go somewhere different. It was one of the reasons she wanted to join the WAAF, to see other parts of the country.'

'Come on, ain't you two finished that barrowful yet?' Nancy said, arriving with another wheelbarrow piled high with compost that she'd ferried over from the heaps on the other side of the garden.

'We're nearly done!' Flo gave Nancy a cheeky look. 'I've been working so hard that I got too hot and had to take my coat off.' She pointed to where it hung on the fence.

'Just as well we're doing this today to keep us warm.'

Nancy, who was an evacuee East Ender billeted with Thea's sister, Prue, had become part of the Rookery House gardening team after Alice left. 'Remember, this is my first winter working outside. I ain't used to the cold.' She let out a laugh. 'But I'd rather be doing this work than anything else.'

'We're glad to have you working alongside us.' Thea gave Nancy a generous smile. 'We were just talking about Alice now working as a Wireless Operator, it's a big change from working here.'

'From what Prue says, her Alice is loving it. She said she wanted to do something practical, and she is. If it were me, I'd be pressing all the wrong buttons and getting in a right mess!'

'Same with me,' Flo agreed. 'But give me a seed and some soil and I know what to do.' She was exactly where she wanted to be and where she needed to be, she thought. She was growing things. It made her happy and contented and working alongside friends like Thea and Nancy was a wonderful bonus, too.

CHAPTER 7

Evie was in the nurses' sitting room waiting for the Wednesday morning briefing to begin. It was the same routine at the start of every shift, when the incoming staff would be updated on the patients' conditions and receive their orders from Matron Reed. It was also an opportunity for Matron to inspect each nurse, checking she was dressed as she should be, her uniform immaculate and her veil neat, pleated and positioned correctly.

'Do I look all right?' Hazel whispered.

Evie looked her friend up and down, taking care to check the impractical white veil was firmly pinned onto Hazel's head. 'I can't see anything to fault.' She lowered her voice. 'But then I'm not Matron!'

'It doesn't matter how many times I've waited here like this, I still get an awful fluttering feeling in my tummy.' Hazel placed her hand over her stomach. 'I worry that something's out of place and I'll be in for a ticking off.'

Evie nodded, giving her friend a sympathetic smile. 'I think we all do.' She glanced around at the other nurses waiting.

'There isn't one of us who hasn't been reprimanded at a morning briefing. We're all glad to get it over and done with so we can get on with looking after our patients. I...' Evie stopped talking at the sound of brisk footsteps approaching in the corridor outside. 'Here she comes.'

The nurses quickly formed themselves into a line standing with their hands clasped in front of them, ready for inspection and to receive today's orders. Evie was aware of how the atmosphere changed, the air prickling with expectation and apprehension.

The door opened and Matron Reed walked in, her shrewd brown eyes scanning the line-up of nurses, checking their uniforms and presentation. Thankfully for everyone this morning, she had no cause to pick up on anything wrong on this occasion.

'Good morning. I'm pleased to say all our patients passed a restful night and are in fine spirits today. If the rain holds off, several of the men can get outside for some fresh air. But before that, there's plenty to be done. Nurse Robertson and Nurse Jones.' Matron directed her gaze at Hazel and Evie. 'You will do the dressings this morning.'

'Yes Matron,' they chorused.

Evie was relieved to have been assigned that task. It was one she didn't mind doing, although she knew that not all the nurses felt the same. She half-listened as Matron continued to give out orders to the others, thinking through what she needed to prepare for the dressings trolley before she could go onto the ward. She might have done it many times before, but never took it for granted because a simple mistake like missing out an essential piece of equipment could be dangerous for a patient.

Matron clapped her hands. 'Right, let's get to work.'

Without waiting for any response, she turned and left the room.

'Shall I do the dressings in Dining Room Ward and you do Library Ward?' Evie asked as she and Hazel headed out of the door, turning left along the corridor towards the servants' area of the Hall and the room where the equipment and supplies for the job were kept.

'Yes, that's fine,' Hazel agreed. 'I don't mind which ward I do. I'm grateful neither of us was sent to work in the sluice this morning.' She gave a mock shudder. '*Nobody* wants to be tasked with working in there if they can help it!'

'But that's exactly where Matron sent each of us when we arrived,' Evie reminded her friend.

She recalled her first few days working here after being transferred to Great Plumstead Hall Hospital from The Millbank hospital in London. Evie had already had plenty of experience working with patients on the wards but Matron Reed had disregarded that, preferring to test and assess Evie's competence for herself, and had assigned her the task of working in the sluice, scrubbing bed pans and urine bottles. It was a basic job usually given to beginner VADs, not experienced ones who could be more useful nursing patients. But Evie had had enough encounters with tricky matrons to know not to argue – instead she knew she must prove herself through hard work and dedication until she was allowed to practise her nursing skills more enjoyably by working on the wards.

'I remember,' Hazel said. 'And we also know we can easily end up back in the sluice if we do something Matron disapproves of!'

'Then let's not make today one of those days,' Evie said brightly. 'We will do the best dressings this place has ever seen!'

As Evie pushed the dressings trolley towards Flight Sergeant Parish's bed, she took a moment to assess how he was this morning. She'd been taught that observation of a patient before beginning what could be a painful procedure for them was vitally important. If they ever looked tired, it might indicate that they'd had a terrible night's sleep and be less amenable or able to tolerate keeping still for any length of time, or bear so much pain. But thankfully, Flight Sergeant Parish was looking bright-eyed and cheerful.

'Good morning.' Evie smiled warmly as she parked the trolley at the foot of his bed. 'How are you today?'

'I'm fine, thank you, Nurse Jones. How are you?' he asked.

'Very well, thank you. I've come to change your dressing.' She raised her eyebrows questioningly, as if asking for his permission.

He grimaced but said firmly, 'It's got to be done and you are the best nurse at doing it. So let's get started, I'm ready when you are.'

Evie patted his arm, appreciating his words and stoic attitude. 'I promise to be as gentle as I can.'

Evie cast her eye over the dressings trolley one last time to double check she had everything she needed and all was in order. It was, and she felt her training and experience taking over as she began. Since she'd become a nurse, Evie had come to understand that some patients liked to chat as she worked, while others preferred to remain silent. Flight Sergeant Parish was one of the quiet ones, seeming to disappear into himself, his eyes either closed or looking up at some distant spot on the ceiling, his breath slow and steady. It was his way of coping and she respected that.

'Are you ready?' she asked.

He nodded.

'You let me know if you need me to stop.'

He gave another brief bob of his head in acknowledgement and shut his eyes.

Evie got to work, taking great care to go carefully and methodically, first removing the soiled dressing and then inspecting the wound, which was healing well. She frequently checked Flight Sergeant Parish's face to see how he was feeling, but his expression remained calm and showed no sign of discomfort. Ready to apply a clean dressing, she took a pair of forceps from the jar of disinfectant and used them to open the lid of the metal drum which contained the sterilised gauze. Taking one out, she quickly closed the top again, then applied the dressing to the wound and bandaged it in place.

'There,' she said when she'd finished, 'how was that?'

Flight Sergeant Parish opened his eyes and gave her a broad grin. 'I told you that you were the best and you've proven it once again. Thank you.'

'I'm glad it was all right for you.'

He looked thoughtful for a moment. 'After what could have happened to me, I promised myself that I wouldn't moan about this.' He waved his hand towards what remained of his right leg. 'I got off lightly compared with the rest of my crew. I'm still here and they're not.'

Sensing that he wanted to talk, Evie pulled up a chair and sat down beside him. In the five days since he'd arrived here, he hadn't spoken about how he had sustained his injuries, something some patients were more open about than others. But when someone was ready to discuss it, then Evie always took the time to listen. She believed talking was as much a part of their recovery as the healing of their physical wounds.

'What happened?' she asked gently.

'We were coming back from a raid and our Lancaster was

in a bad way. We were lucky to make it as far as our aerodrome and hoped we could get her down in one piece. And we nearly did, but something went wrong... and we crashed. I was the only crew member who survived.' He shook his head, tears welling up in his eyes.

Evie took hold of his hand in hers. 'I'm sorry.'

He gave a small, sad smile. 'We all knew it could happen. It was a risk we took every single time we got in that plane. But we still did it.' He drew in a deep breath. 'I'm grateful I am still here, because I could easily not have been. I might have lost some of my leg but I didn't lose my life that day.'

'Once you're up and mobile and your leg is fully healed, you'll be fitted with an artificial limb and soon be able to walk about again,' Evie said. 'We'll get you ready for that as quick as we can.'

'Want to be rid of me already?' His eyes twinkled with mirth.

'Oh, I think we can put up with you for a little while longer,' Evie retorted with a laugh.

CHAPTER 8

Stepping through the gap in the blackout curtain into the light-filled village hall felt especially welcoming tonight, Flo thought, as she shrugged off her coat, which sparkled with tiny water droplets from the chilly drizzle outside.

'Give me your coat as well and I'll hang them where they can dry,' she told Hettie.

'Thank you,' Hettie replied. 'I'll get us seats.'

Flo and Hettie had bicycled together from Rookery House for the regular Thursday evening meeting of Great Plumstead's village singing group. Coming here each week to sing alongside other women under the guidance of Gloria was always a joy, and worth turning out for on a cold winter's night.

After hanging her and Hettie's coats on pegs near the door, Flo joined the other women who were sitting in a semi-circle of chairs arranged in the centre of the hall. She greeted the others and then sat down next to Hettie, who'd found them seats beside Prue.

'Good evening, everyone! Welcome to tonight's singing group,' Gloria said, standing in front of them with her arms out in greeting. Tonight, she was wearing her poppy-red dress, which was a burst of colour bright enough to liven up any room. 'Before we warm up our voices, I 'ave some exciting news to share with you...' she beamed, her eyes scanning over the group. 'Lady Campbell-Gryce 'as asked us to put on a carol concert for the patients at Great Plumstead Hall 'ospital to 'elp make their stay in 'ospital more cheery over the festive season.'

Murmurings of approval came from the other singers, but Flo's heart felt as if it had suddenly been gripped by an icy-cold hand.

'When would the concert be?' Prue asked.

'On Tuesday the twenty-second, that's close enough to Christmas to be festive but not impinge on all the other things us women need to get done,' Gloria replied.

Flo sat silent and still, her whole body frozen as if she were sculpted from marble. She was aware of the others chattering excitedly around her, the news of the concert having been heartily received by everyone. Except her. A carol concert on the anniversary of her family's death in the Manchester Blitz was something she couldn't ever be involved in. For one thing she no longer sang Christmas carols. The last time she'd sung any was shortly before the air-raid siren had gone. She'd been enjoying her absolute favourite, *The Holly and the Ivy*. Minutes later, her family's home lay in rubble with her parents, brother and sister dead inside it. Ever since then, Flo had associated carols with that terrible night that had brought her such pain and heartbreak. How could she possibly sing them again with the joy and warmth they were meant to express?

'Flo?' Hettie's voice broke into her thoughts. 'Are you feeling all right? Only you've gone pale.'

Flo looked at her friend, whose eyes behind her round

36

glasses were full of concern. 'I've got a headache starting. I'll just get a drink of water.' She stood up and hurried into the kitchen adjoining the main hall, glad to escape and give herself a chance to think.

Taking her time to find a cup and fill it with cold water from the tap, Flo could hear the others going through the warm-up routine led by Gloria. Their voices rising from low to high, they hummed and la-laaed their way through practice tunes, each exercise gently stretching their vocal cords in preparation for singing. It was always a process accompanied by eruptions of giggling at the amusing sounds they made. Flo felt strange listening from a distance, removed from her friends. But then that was how it had to be now because Flo simply could not join them singing carols.

The warm-up finished, she heard Gloria say something about borrowed hymn books and asking for them to be given out. Flo lingered in the kitchen, sipping at her water, wondering how much longer she could hide in here, when Gloria appeared in the doorway.

'Are you all right, Flo? Hettie said you've got an 'eadache – do you want to take an aspirin tablet for it? I've got some in my 'andbag.'

Flo shook her head. 'It's not that bad, I just...' she halted, not wanting to voice her feelings aloud.

'What is it, ducks? Maybe I can 'elp? It ain't like you to not want to join in. You're one of my best voices. Was it something I said?' Gloria came over and put her hand on Flo's arm.

Flo stared down at her feet for a few moments. She wanted to tell Gloria, in fact she owed it to her friend who'd encouraged her to join the singing group last year, and since then it had brought Flo a lot of joy.

She looked up and met Gloria's eyes. 'It's the carols. I just can't sing them any more because... because they remind me of the night my family was killed. I was singing some just before the siren went and...' She couldn't finish and bowed her head as Gloria wrapped her in a tight, perfumy embrace.

'I'm so sorry to bring that memory up for you, ducks.' Gloria stepped back, keeping her hands on Flo's upper arms. 'You don't 'ave to sing what ain't right for you. I'd planned to rehearse for the Christmas performance before our tea break and then after tea we'll move on to some of the songs we usually sing. If you want to sit out this first bit, then do.'

Flo's eyes filled with tears. 'Thank you. I'll make myself useful in here and get the tea things ready while you rehearse. I know it sounds silly not wanting to sing carols...'

'There ain't nothing silly about it. What 'appened to you was terrible and it's left a scar that's 'ard to live with. Now you stay in 'ere if you want and I'll go and see 'ow we get on with a festive medley. I've borrowed hymn books from the vicar so we'll all know the right words. I don't want any *shepherds washing their socks* by night.' She rolled her eyes. 'I know we all used to sing that at school, but if we're going to be performing at the 'ospital in front of Lady Campbell-Gryce, then we need to do it properly. All right, ducks?'

Flo nodded. 'I'll join in again after the tea break.'

Gloria gave her an understanding smile. 'Good. I'll see you again shortly.'

Flo watched Gloria return to the hall, her high heels tip-tapping as she went, then listened as her friend instructed the singing group to turn to page 136 in the hymn book ready for *While Shepherds Watched*. Followed by a reminder that it was *watched flocks*, not washed socks, and to sing the words printed in the hymn book. Flo found herself laughing, grateful for her wonderful friend's kindness and understanding.

Setting out the teacups on the trolley, Flo listened to the familiar songs, and to her surprise, she found herself enjoying them. But listening was one thing. Singing them herself was another matter altogether.

CHAPTER 9

Shrieks of laughter were coming down the hallway of Prue's house as Thea let herself in through the front door. She'd tried knocking, but there hadn't been an answer, and it wasn't any wonder from the amount of noise spilling out from inside the workroom. No one in there would have heard her rattling the door knocker. Smiling to herself at the change of atmosphere in the house from how it used to be when Prue's husband Victor had ruled the roost, Thea made her way to what was once Victor's study. It had now been transformed into a workroom for use by the women of The Mother's Day Club, where they could carry out sewing or knitting tasks such as making clothes for the village clothing depot.

Peering around the door, Thea spotted the source of the hilarity. Her sister Prue stood in the middle of the room with a pink floral-patterned curtain draped around her, which Gloria was pinning into place in the shape of a dress.

'There, that should do it.' Gloria stepped back and stood with one hand on her hip, looking her friend up and down. 'What do you think ladies? 'Ow does that look?'

Prue rolled her eyes, laughing as the other women clapped and shouted out their approval.

Spotting Thea standing in the doorway, her sister called out to her. 'Come and rescue me, do, before I end up with a dress that would look far better on somebody else than me.'

'You underestimate yourself,' Gloria said, shaking her head. 'You always stick to safe plain colours when I 'onestly think something brighter and more colourful would suit you far better.'

'Maybe,' Prue conceded. 'But right now, the clothes I already have must suffice. There's a war on, don't forget, and this curtain will make some lovely girls' dresses for our depot.' She began to unpin the fabric, with Thea and Gloria bending down to help.

'Fair enough, but I won't forget and I'll 'ave you wearing something more colourful one day!' Gloria warned her, with a mischievous grin, her eyes sparkling with amusement under her blonde pompadour hairstyle. 'What about you, Thea? Can I tempt you into wearing something more exotic?'

Thea looked down at her dark green dungarees which were perfectly suited to her work in the garden at Rookery House. 'I'm not sure I have the need for anything like that right now but thank you for your kind offer, Gloria.'

'Oh well, some lucky little ladies in this village are going to be delighted with new dresses made from this.' Gloria folded up the unpinned curtain and draped it over one arm. 'If we get a shift on we might even be able to get them made in time for Christmas!'

'I appreciate you thinking of me,' Prue told Gloria, 'I really do. One day, I'll consider taking you up on it.'

'Hear that, ladies?' Gloria looked round at the other women who'd paused their work at the tables and sewing machines to watch the antics. 'You are all my witnesses and we'll 'old Prue to that, won't we? She'd look smashing in a raspberry pink like this.' She held up the curtain before turning to Prue, adding, 'It complements your complexion and hair beautifully.'

'One day,' Prue said, giving Gloria's free hand a squeeze before turning to her sister. 'Have you come to help us? We've just had another delivery of holey airmen's socks from RAF Great Plumstead if you fancied doing some darning.'

Thea laughed. 'I think if I did some, the owners would wish I hadn't bothered. Darning was never my strong point! Have you got a minute because I need to ask you something?'

'Of course, come through to the kitchen. We're going to stop for a tea break soon anyway so I'll put the kettle on while we talk.'

Thea followed her sister into the kitchen. 'It looks like you have a lot of fun in that workroom.'

Prue nodded as she pushed the kettle on to the hot plate of the stove to boil. 'We do, and we get plenty of work done, too. It's an excellent combination of fun and effort and has made a tremendous difference to the amount of clothes we can make. The clothing depot has a much healthier stock now than it used to.' She paused, looking thoughtful. 'I love that a room I used to dread going into has become a place of laughter and friendship – *and* helps the community. This time last year I couldn't have imagined such a thing.' She gave a small shake of her head. 'My world has changed, and in so many ways for the better.'

Thea's eyes met her sister's and a look of understanding passed between them. Since Prue's husband had been killed in the Norwich Blitz back in April, her life had altered dramatically. While most widows would have been mourning the tragic loss of their husbands, for Prue it had been a release as her marriage hadn't ever been a happy one. Victor had been a controlling and domineering man who'd only married Prue so she could look after his children rather than having to pay someone to do it after his first wife died. What most people didn't know was that Victor had been killed in the home of his mistress. It was a fact that the wider community would have been horrified to learn because he had cultivated the image of an upstanding businessman, member of numerous committees and part of the Home Guard.

Now Prue's life was much happier and her decision to turn what had once been Victor's study into the workroom was an inspired one. It benefited so many and also helped Prue lay the ghost of her late husband's presence to rest.

'What is it you wanted to speak to me about?' Prue asked, putting some cups on a tray.

'I was wondering what your plans were for Christmas Day?' Thea said. 'Only we'd all like it if you, Nancy and the girls would join us at Rookery House. Lizzie's coming from Norwich as usual and Reuben will be there. What do you think?'

Prue smiled. 'It's good of you to ask us all. Thank you. I can't give you a firm answer until I've spoken to Nancy. It wouldn't be right to decide on her behalf though I know she'll appreciate the offer.'

'That's fair enough,' Thea agreed. 'Just tell me when you're ready. There will be plenty of food. And I hope you can come, but if you'd prefer not to, that's fine, too. You must do what feels best for you, especially as it will be the first Christmas since Victor died and you might want to spend it here doing things your way.'

'I promise I'll let you know after I've spoken to Nancy. Now, will you join us for a cup of tea?'

Thea glanced at her watch. 'I'd better not. I came into the village to deliver the vegetables to Barker's grocers and only popped in here on the off chance that you were at home. I've left Flo and Nancy cleaning out the greenhouse and need to get back to help.'

Leaving her sister to make the tea, Thea could hear more chatter and laughter coming from the workroom as she headed for the front door. It was such a delight to see and hear what a transformation Prue had brought about in the past few months both in this house and herself. After years of worrying about her sister, Thea felt happier about her than she had for a very long time.

CHAPTER 10

Evie's monthly weekends off from her work at the hospital had become even more precious to her since she and Ned had become a couple last December. Apart from Saturday mornings when he was required to work in the gardens at Great Plumstead Hall, the rest of the weekend they could be together as much as possible. How they spent that time varied depending on the season or what other events were happening.

Today they were in Wykeham having bicycled in, the chill air turning their cheeks a rosy pink by the time they'd reached the small town. After stowing their bicycles in the back yard of Wilson's Seed and Agricultural merchant, which was owned by Prue and her family, they'd paid a visit to the bookshop, followed by afternoon tea in the cafe overlooking the market square. Now they were having a stroll by the river before they headed back to Rookery House.

Stopping under the sweeping boughs of a weeping willow growing on the bank, they watched a swan glide majestically by.

'Isn't he or she beautiful?' Evie said, noticing how the bird's webbed feet propelled it along in a rhythmical motion just beneath the surface. 'I love how it looks so graceful and serene above but is paddling away under the water.'

'Some people are like that,' Ned commented. 'Looking calm and collected on the outside, while inside, they're in turmoil. Others show everything they're feeling on their faces. If they're sad, you know about it. The same if they are happy. Then there are all ways in between, like on a sliding scale.'

'What about you?' Evie asked. 'Where do you sit on that scale, then? You always seem calm to me, but is there a hidden whirlpool of confusion and turbulent thoughts going on inside you?' She raised an eyebrow, looking at him as she waited for his answer.

'What do you think?'

'Umm,' Evie put her head on one side. 'I may be wrong, but I think you are a calm, steady person all the way through. You usually think carefully about things before you act. You're not boiling with turmoil underneath and neither are you the sort who, if he's sad, makes others feel bad around him. That's how...' Her words juddered to a halt as an image of her late husband Douglas flashed into her mind – of him in a temper and making sure she felt the wrath of it. It was an unwelcome reminder of what she'd endured throughout her miserable marriage.

Ned's face clouded as he realised what she might be thinking. 'I'm sorry. I didn't mean to bring back bad memories.' He pulled her into his arms and held her tight.

Evie rested her head on his chest and felt her shoulders relax. 'It's all right, you did nothing. Sometimes a memory will pop up when I least expect it. Or want it.' She stepped back and looked into Ned's kind eyes. 'Let's not allow it to spoil our time together. We don't get enough of it and it's my weekend off so we must enjoy it.'

'I wish we could be together more.' Ned's eyes locked with hers and they stared at each other in silence for a few moments before he suddenly went down onto one knee in front of her and took hold of her hand. 'Will you marry me, Evie? It would make me the happiest of men and I promise to *always* love and care for you for the rest of my life.'

Evie put her free hand to her mouth, her stomach dropping like a stone to the muddy bottom of the river, as Ned gazed up at her, his eyes full of hope.

'What do you think? We could be together a lot more if we were married,' Ned encouraged her.

Tears prickled the back of Evie's eyes; she hadn't expected this. She didn't *want* this to happen. 'Why now?' she asked.

'I've been thinking about it for a while,' Ned said. 'I wasn't planning on asking you today but … Evie, I want to take care of you, and we could be with each other so much more if we were married. Say something Evie, put me out of my misery down here.' He smiled at her.

'You've surprised me and I need time to think about it. I'm sorry, but I can't give you an answer now.' Because going by her gut reaction to his proposal, it would probably be no, Evie thought.

Ned got to his feet, taking her free hand so he now held both of hers in his. 'I understand. I've sprung it on you. Take all the time you need.' He kissed her gently. 'I hope when you're ready that you'll say yes.'

Evie forced herself to smile. Their lovely day out had just taken a dramatic and unwanted turn. Why had he gone and spoilt it by asking her a question that she never wanted to hear again?

Evie found herself avoiding Ned's gaze. 'We need to head

back to Rookery House before it gets dark,' she said, taking a step back in the direction they'd come. Ned let go of her hands and she quickly linked an arm through his. 'It was just such a surprise,' she repeated kindly, never wanting to hurt him, not her Ned.

As they walked along the river path towards the centre of Wykeham to collect their bicycles, Evie's mind was spinning with confusion. She loved Ned very much, but his sudden proposal and desire for them to be married may have ruined everything between them. If she couldn't give him the answer he hoped for then where would it leave them?

CHAPTER 11

It was Saturday afternoon and Flo was standing at the far side of Five Acres field, a spot as distant as she could get from Rookery House and still be on Thea's land. Beyond the hedge was another field with only the remaining pale-yellow stubble from the stalks of this year's wheat harvest poking up from the brown soil. Rooks were picking their way across it, probing their beaks into the earth searching for grubs. Apart from the birds, Flo was alone. If she was going to try, then this was the time and place to do it.

The idea had been niggling at her since this week's singing practice, growing more insistent until she had no option but to do something about it. Either she would prove herself right, or else surprise herself. Flo had to give it a go. If nothing else, it would stop the niggling feeling and she would know for sure one way or the other.

What to start with? she wondered. Which carol should she try? Definitely not… she sharply nipped that thought in the bud. She couldn't sing that one ever again! No, she needed to begin with something else, something less emotionally connected to her.

Closing her eyes, she took a few slow, deep breaths and started softly humming the notes of *Once in Royal David's City*, saying the words to the tune in her head. It felt familiar and safe. Opening her mouth, she tried singing in a hushed voice, testing the words out for shape and sound. Keeping her eyes closed, she focused on how the notes resonated in her chest and throat. Tears welled in her eyes, but she squeezed her lids tighter to stop them falling. Raising her voice slightly, she moved on to *Away in a Manger*.

Little by little, Flo felt herself relax. Her shoulders settled and a warmth spread through her as she sang the age-old words that she'd given voice to so many times before, right from when she was a young child. Christmas carols had always been some of her favourite songs to sing. There was something about the familiar, rich and uplifting melodies that fully brought to life such a special time of year. One which her family had always enjoyed and looked forward to.

She had just started *O Come All Ye Faithful*, letting her voice grow stronger, when she heard a small bark and felt a wet nudge against her hand. Snapping her eyes open she saw Bess, Reuben's dog, standing in front of her. The collie was wagging her tail and looking up at Flo with eager amber eyes.

'Bess, what are you doing here?' Flo patted the dog's head, realising that Reuben must be nearby as his faithful companion never strayed far from him. Turning, she spotted Thea's brother walking towards her along the side of the field. He put up his hand in greeting.

Had he heard her? she wondered. And what should she say she was doing? Standing out here by a hedge and singing with eyes closed wasn't exactly the usual thing to be doing and would require an explanation of some kind.

'You've got a lovely voice,' Reuben said as he approached. 'Are you practising for the Christmas concert? I heard there's going to be one at the hospital.'

Flo's cheeks grew warm – so he *had* heard her. 'I wasn't sure if I could sing carols again...' The words tumbled out before she could stop them.

'Why's that?' he asked curiously, stroking Bess's ears as the dog was now sitting close by him, leaning against his legs.

'I haven't sung them since...' she put her hand to her mouth as tears welled up in her eyes again. 'Since the night my family was killed. I was singing them just before the siren went. I was supposed to go out carolling the following evening with some others from work to raise money for the Red Cross.'

'And so now you associate singing carols with that night,' Reuben said gently.

Flo nodded. 'Last year was the first Christmas since I lost everyone, and when the carols started, I just couldn't bring myself to join in. It brought back such terrible memories.' She took a deep breath, looking for a moment towards the house where she could see George and Betty running around in the garden playing some game with Thea. 'On Thursday when Gloria told us we were going to be doing a carol concert at the hospital, well...' She folded her arms across her front. 'It stirred things up in me again. Gloria understood and said I must do what I'm comfortable with, but it's made me think, am I going to have to avoid something I used to love for the rest of my life?'

Reuben's face was sympathetic. When he spoke, his voice was thickened by emotion. 'I was like that with cricket.'

Flo frowned. 'Cricket?'

'Yes, after the Great War, when I got home, I didn't want to take part in or even think about cricket ever again. It had been what my brother William and I did together, the one thing that most bound us. We both played for the village and there was a great rivalry with other local teams. We had lived for those Saturday afternoons; they were the highlight of our summers as young men.'

Rueben took off his weather-stained cap and passed a hand through his thick greying hair. He looked down at Bess and stroked her ears, then lifted his gaze back to Flo. 'I felt like I could never get out there on the crease again. Because William couldn't, not anymore. But then I realised that it was the one thing he'd want me to do. Help our team. He'd have had strong words to say to me if I didn't put my all into helping Great Plumstead win at cricket. So I started playing again and still do. For me. And for William.'

'I remember you telling me about your brother.' Flo's eyes met Reuben's. 'How you felt guilty about surviving when he didn't, and how you try to live well for him.'

'I do. It's not always easy, but time has helped ease the pain. You never forget the ones you lose.' Reuben let out a soft sigh. 'We carry them with us.' He paused then asked, 'You seemed to be able to sing carols just now. Do you think you could sing them in public?'

Flo considered for a few moments, Reuben's words about his brother seeming to help her see a way forward. 'I think so. Maybe not all of them, but some.'

'Then that's a good start. You could try it out at the singing group, see how it goes. If you're not ready, then you don't have to take part in the concert, not if it doesn't feel right. Go one step at a time.' He nodded his head towards the birds in the next field. 'I'm sure the rooks enjoyed your singing, and Bess and I did too. We'd have listened longer if Bess hadn't been so keen to join in!'

Flo laughed. 'Thank you – *both* of you. It was hard to try

but I'm glad I came out here today and sang for you all. And you're right, I need to take it one thing at a time and see where it leads me.'

Reuben replaced his cap. 'I'll leave you to it. Come on, Bess.' He turned and headed off in the direction of his railway carriage home in Thea's back garden.

Flo watched him go, thinking how much she liked Thea's brother. He was a quiet man who didn't say much, but when he did, it was always worth listening to. Despite her initial dismay at him hearing her singing, she was glad he had. She had inadvertently broken the invisible barrier of singing carols and being heard. There was no reason for her not to try it again with the singing group.

Although there was still one carol she wasn't prepared to sing. That would be too much.

CHAPTER 12

Evie couldn't sleep. She lay staring upwards in the direction of the ceiling in the pitch black of her bedroom. No matter how hard she tried, she just could not get Ned's proposal out of her mind. She desperately wished he hadn't asked her.

'Can't you sleep either?' Flo's voice came through the darkness.

Evie heard her friend shift in her bed, then plump up her pillow. 'No, I wish I could,' she replied. 'Why aren't you asleep by now?'

'I've been thinking about this carol concert at the hospital that the singing group's been asked to do. It's stirred up a lot of memories and I don't know if I can take part in it. I haven't sung any carols since my family was killed but today...' Flo's voice wavered. 'I tried singing some carols away from the house, on my own out at the far side of Five Acres and... it was all right. I managed it. But that was thinking I was on my own. I'm not yet sure if I could sing them with other people in the singing group, let alone in front of an audience at the Hall...'

Evie rolled onto her side, facing Flo, although she couldn't see her friend in the blackness. 'It was a good idea to test things on your own first. The only way to find out if you *can* sing carols with the group is to try. It might not be easy for you to begin with, but you'll never know if you can do it unless you give it a go.'

'When you say it like that, it makes perfect sense, but singing with thoughts and feelings churning inside me it becomes far more complicated. I worry that I might not be able to hold myself together, and then the experience will set me back rather than helping me take a step forward.'

'I understand. So why not try it out, just in the safety of your singing group, with your wonderful friends there to support you? I'm sure they'll be on your side and keen to help. And just start by joining in with one verse of a carol, one line, a single word even? Break it down into tiny bits. And if at any time you can't carry on, then you can stop,' Evie suggested. 'You have a good reason to not want to sing carols again, if that's how it turns out.'

'Part of me thinks it would be a terrible shame to never sing carols again, as they should be sung – with others, enjoying the spirit and joy of Christmas together.' Flo fell silent for a moment before asking, 'What's keeping you awake?'

'Ned proposed to me today,' Evie said in a flat voice.

'What!' Flo exclaimed across the short distance between their beds. 'What did you tell him?'

'I told him I need to think about it, but...' Evie's voice tailed off as the turmoil in her mind looped round and round, the same questions filling her head and the different scenarios of what might happen if she did this or that playing out.

'Do you *want* to marry him?'

'No!' There, she'd said it out loud, Evie thought. She had

55

voiced her gut reaction to Ned's proposal. 'I don't want to marry anyone ever again. I did it once and look where it got me. After that, I've sworn to never make the same mistake.'

'But Ned's not anything like Douglas, is he?'

'No, he isn't. Otherwise, I wouldn't be with him at all.' Evie had confided in Flo about her disastrous marriage to Douglas during their chats as roommates. She'd told her of the many times he'd hit her, how he had tormented her with his words, stopping her from seeing her friends, shrinking her world into one dominated by him and his rules and wants. It had only been his joining the army and leaving her alone at home in London that had allowed her to secretly take nursing courses. Then, when he was posted abroad, to work as a VAD nurse in a London hospital. After narrowly avoiding being killed in an air raid during the Blitz, Evie had faked her own death and escaped to Norfolk to start work at Great Plumstead Hall Hospital and come to live here at Rookery House. Douglas had been killed in action in North Africa some months later, and she had finally been free of him.

'I'm sure Ned would never treat you like Douglas did,' Flo said, interrupting Evie's thoughts, which had inevitably taken her back to those awful days of her marriage.

'I would hope not. The problem is, I never thought Douglas would either. Before we got married, he was kind and caring and I loved him. I had no idea he had another, horrible side or else I wouldn't have married him, no matter if it was a good match which my mother approved of, with him coming from such a wealthy family. As I discovered to my cost, being from a grand heritage doesn't mean a person behaves decently.' Evie let out a heavy sigh. 'It was marriage that changed things. Do you see? I love Ned, but I could never marry him.'

'What will happen if you say no?'

'I'm not sure … I just don't know.' She hesitated before voicing the thought that had been tormenting her, unable now to control her sobs. 'But how can I even be with him, knowing that I can never give him what he wants? Could anyone be so cruel?'

A rustling of covers signalled her friend leaping out of bed; she felt Flo's warm hands reaching out in the darkness to take hold of hers.

'What a tangled web of questions Ned has created by proposing to you,' Flo said gently, squeezing Evie's hands in hers. 'But you're a strong woman and you know your own mind and heart and are brave enough to listen to what they tell you. And if that's never to marry again, then you must do what's right for you. I will always support you.'

'Thank you. I don't know what's going to happen and I'm sad that things will probably change between Ned and I, and for the worse, I fear. I wish he'd never asked me.'

There was no turning back the clock, Evie thought. The question had been posed and she owed it to Ned to give him an answer. She wished there was another way to stay true to herself and yet give Ned what he hoped for. But that was impossible, wasn't it?

CHAPTER 13

The days were getting shorter and it didn't help that this afternoon the heavy grey clouds tipping out rain were making the light fade even earlier than usual. But then it was almost mid-December, Thea thought, and to be expected. At least the shortened afternoons gave her a good reason to be indoors, snug and warm by the fire and enjoying some welcome company with friends and family. Resisting the urge to draw the curtains of the sitting room and block out the miserable weather, which would only make the winter's night seem that much longer, she returned her attention to the conversation going on around her.

'Do you remember taking part in the school nativity play?' Hettie asked, directing her question to Ted who'd been on Home Guard duty with Reuben that morning and the pair of them had been invited to join in Sunday roast dinner at Rookery House.

'I do. I got to be the innkeeper one year. It was the highlight of the term for me, even if I forgot my lines on the day.' Ted laughed.

'I remember when Reuben played the Angel Gabriel.' Thea smiled at her brother, who rolled his eyes in response.

'I would much rather have been a shepherd,' Reuben admitted. 'You'd never believe it, but back then I had very impressive golden curls and that must have got me the part of the angel. I'm much more the shepherd now.' He gestured at his dark brown hair, which was flecked with silver – all signs of angelic golden curls long ago outgrown.

'*I'm* going to be a shepherd,' George piped up from his seat at the small table where he was playing a game of snakes and ladders with Flo and his sister, Betty.

'And *I'm* an angel,' Betty added, shaking the dice between her cupped hands.

Thea was looking forward to watching George and Betty in their roles. The pair of them were both excited about acting their parts in front of their schoolmates.

'I think they still use some of the costumes we used back then,' Hettie said. 'At last year's nativity, I'm sure I recognised the Three Kings' cloaks from when I was at school. My brother Sidney was a king one year and he loved it.'

'You should come along with us to see it, Ted,' Thea suggested. 'It's in the church on the afternoon of the twenty-second, the day before the children break up for the Christmas holidays on the twenty-third.'

Ted nodded, considering for a moment. 'I'd like that, thank you. It has been a long time since I went to a nativity play, and if George and Betty are taking part, then I know it will be good so I won't want to miss it.'

The children looked delighted with Ted's compliment as they continued playing their game.

Ted finished, 'I'd be happy to join you all.'

'It starts at two o'clock,' Hettie told him. 'We'll save you a seat with us as the church soon fills up.'

As the conversation moved on Thea stole a glance at Hettie, who was happily knitting a glove and seemed fine with her inviting Ted to join them. Ted had become a regular visitor to Rookery House over the past six months, growing to be a friend to Thea, Reuben and everyone who lived here, sharing his experience and knowledge and always willing to join in and help. He'd stepped in on several occasions, volunteering when Nancy couldn't come to work as one or other of her daughters was unwell and she needed to stay at home to care for them. Thea still strongly suspected Ted was sweet on Hettie, but hadn't, so far as Thea knew, pursued his feelings further. Time would tell and, if Thea was honest with herself, she hoped he would, and that Hettie and Ted might become a couple. She thought they were very well suited as a pair, and the kindly Ted was just the sort of partner Hettie deserved.

CHAPTER 14

Flo had finished the afternoon milking, taken the bucket of milk to the house and was filling up Primrose's hayrack in the byre with fresh hay to last the night. Now that the weather was cold and the nights long, the cow remained closed indoors overnight, rather than having free access to the meadow as she did during the warmer months when she could graze from dawn to dusk. Tending to Primrose wasn't one of Flo's regular tasks as Thea liked to do the milking and had a particular bond with their Jersey cow, but today Thea was on duty in the WVS canteen so had given Flo the job in her place.

Singing softly to herself as she worked, Flo found herself swept away by the gentle words and music of *Silent Night*. She knew it was one of the carols the singing group planned to perform at the concert on the twenty-second, and that was probably why her mind conjured it up this afternoon. Since trying out carols for the first time up in Five Acres field on Saturday, Flo had gradually been acclimatising herself to singing more of them whenever she was alone. Singing or even just humming a medley of carols as she went about her work was helping to ease the heavy feeling she'd had about them. She had even sung while she'd milked Primrose and the cow seemed to have approved, letting down her milk easily. By the time the singing group next met in three days' time for their regular Thursday night practise, Flo hoped she could join in with the rest of the women as they rehearsed carols and not need to hide away in the kitchen as she'd done the previous week.

'There, that should keep you going until the morning.' Flo patted Primrose's shoulder. 'Sleep well.'

Leaving the cow munching on hay, Flo left the byre and was closing the door behind her when a small figure came pelting towards her across the garden. It was George and he wasn't long home from school.

'Flo, Flo! Help me!' he stammered out the words as she caught hold of him. 'Flopsy's out and I can't catch her. It's all my fault and Auntie Thea's going to be so angry with me.' His blue eyes welled with tears and they spilt over, running down his flushed cheeks.

Flo bobbed down on her heels so that her face was level with his, her heart aching at seeing the little boy so upset. 'What happened?'

'I had Flopsy out of the run. She was sitting on my lap and I was stroking her and then a plane went over and it made her jump. She ran off and I've tried to catch her, but every time I get nearly close enough, she hops off a bit further.' More tears rolled down his face. 'I know I shouldn't have had her out on my own but I just wanted to talk to her and stroke her. I didn't mean for this to happen. The fox might catch her!'

'It's all right. We'll find Flopsy.' Flo stood up and held out her hand to the little boy. 'Come on, show me where you think she is.' Flo tried to sound more optimistic than she felt.

The rabbit might have wandered off while George came to fetch her. 'Where did you last see her?'

'Near the greenhouse. She was nibbling on the plantain growing there.'

'Right, we'll go there first.'

Approaching the greenhouse, Flo was relieved to see that Flopsy hadn't gone far and was still enjoying the patch of plantain she'd discovered. But there was still a good chance she might run again and this time head for thicker cover. The best thing to do was to limit how far she could go. The rabbit, who was usually very docile and friendly, had simply got a new sense of freedom and wanted to explore and find tasty things to eat.

'We need to take things slowly and mustn't startle her,' Flo warned George. 'I'm going to open the greenhouse door and if we can gradually encourage her to go inside, then it will be easier to pick her up in there.'

Walking around in a wider arc to avoid startling the rabbit, Flo reached the greenhouse and opened the door. Then she made her way back so that she and George were between Flopsy and the wider garden. 'Now spread your arms out like me,' Flo demonstrated, 'and take tiny steps towards her. Don't scare her. Just gently guide her towards the greenhouse.'

Together the pair of them moved inch by inch towards the rabbit, who although she was still eating, her nose and whiskers twitching as she chewed, kept her eyes on them. As they drew nearer Flopsy hopped away from them, getting closer and closer to the open greenhouse until, with a large bound, she leapt inside.

Flo darted forward, followed by George; they slipped inside the greenhouse and closed the door behind them. 'There,' Flo said, smiling at the little boy, who looked as relieved as she felt. 'Now she can't go anywhere. You stay in here with her while I fetch a couple of cabbage leaves to tempt her. Whatever you do, *don't open the door!*'

'I won't,' George promised.

'I shan't be long.' Flo slipped out of the greenhouse, quickly securing the door behind her, and hurried to one of the vegetable patches where some winter cabbages were growing. Chuckling to herself, she snapped off enough leaves to placate even the most determined of adventurous rabbits, then headed back.

The sight that met her made her heart ache all over again, and she felt a prickle of tears stinging her eyes. Not unhappy tears, she thought, watching George, who was sitting cross-legged in the middle of the greenhouse floor with the white-and-brown rabbit on his lap. The rabbit's eyelids were closed in quiet contentment as George stroked her back and ears.

Flo let herself in quietly. 'Well done, George!' she whispered to him.

'She came over to me when I sat down,' George said, looking up at Flo and beaming.

'That's good. She knows how well you care for her.' Flo sat next to him and handed him the cabbage leaves, which Flopsy must have smelt as she opened her eyes and began to nibble the one George offered her.

'Why did she run away from me?' he asked.

'Probably because there was so much to explore. But she came back to you in here. She knows and trusts you.' Flo reached out and stroked the rabbit's soft, delicate fur.

'Do you think Auntie Thea will be cross with me for letting her run off? I know I shouldn't have got her out on my own, but I was thinking about Flopsy at school today and wanted to spend time with her.' George's eyes filled with tears again.

Flo put her arm around his shoulders. 'Thea wouldn't be

cross with you. There's no need to worry about that. Flopsy's safe now and all's well that ends well.'

'I won't ever get her out on my own any more in case she does it again,' George said.

'Then it sounds to me like you've learned a lesson from what's happened. You know how easily Flopsy can run off if there's no one else around to help. How about we just keep what happened today between the two of us, because no harm came of it?'

'The *three* of us you mean.' George looked down at the rabbit. 'Flopsy won't say anything and if you think we don't need to tell Auntie Thea, then I won't.'

'It's our secret and it's all turned out well.' Flo put a hand on her heart. 'I promise I won't say anything either.' Her eyes met George's and they both grinned. 'Would you look at that – Flopsy's nearly eaten that cabbage leaf already!'

George giggled and Flo's heart warmed at seeing the little boy happy again, his problem solved and his worries sorted. It reminded her of the times she'd helped her brother Bobby, who'd had a habit of getting up to mischief. It was never anything bad, but his curiosity sometimes got him into trouble, and being his big sister, she'd had the experience to help him fix things before he found himself in hot water with their parents. Like George, Bobby had always learned from his mistakes and it had been a delight to see him grow and mature until… Flo let out a soft sigh. She would always miss her brother and wonder what he would have become if he'd had the chance to grow up. It would always hurt that it could never happen, but Flo was grateful for the privilege of having someone like George in her life, who she'd taken under her wing and helped just as she'd once done with Bobby.

'Right, I think we'd better get Flopsy back to her run.' Flo stood up. 'Hold on to her tightly as you carry her back,' she advised George, watching as he got to his feet, cradling the rabbit securely but gently in his arms. Flo could have insisted that she hold Flopsy but decided it was better for George to take the responsibility and for him to know that she trusted him to do it.

A few minutes later, the rabbit was safely back in her hutch and was munching on the remains of the cabbage leaves. 'There, she's safe and sound.'

'Thank you for helping me.' George wrapped his arms around her and hugged her tightly.

Flo returned his embrace. 'I'm glad I could help. Now, you must be hungry after school. Let's go and see what Hettie's got planned for our tea.'

CHAPTER 15

Evie felt like her hands weren't cooperating this morning, and that, combined with the inability of her mind to focus on the job, was making for a difficult shift. The task she and Hazel had been assigned was one they'd done countless times before. It was a cornerstone of VAD duties and essential for the health and well-being of their patients. Although it might only be a thorough clean of Dining Room Ward, removing all dirt, dust and potentially harmful unhygienic organisms, it was important and a job that Evie normally found satisfying. It certainly wasn't fancy and involved plenty of getting down on her hands and knees scrubbing the floor or washing down bed frames and lockers – however it usually gave her a sense of a worthwhile job well done. Even the monotonous parts could be restful, giving her time to think. Unfortunately, today she wished her thoughts would be quiet and let her get on, only they wouldn't. Ned's surprising proposal and its potential consequences kept going round and round in her head.

Dunking the cloth she was using to wash a bed frame into the bucket of hot soapy water, Evie caught the bucket handle with her elbow and, before she could stop it, the whole thing tipped over. Its contents puddled out across the floor and a strong smell of carbolic soap filled the air.

She stared at the spill in horror, as if frozen to the spot.

'Nurse Jones! What is the meaning of this?' Matron's strident voice made Evie jump, her heart leaping in her chest.

She closed her eyes briefly and let out an almost silent sigh, wondering how Matron had the knack of appearing whenever somebody had done something they shouldn't have.

'Well, don't just sit there staring, get it cleaned up!' Matron's command was laced with impatience. 'What are you playing at this morning? I expect more from you than this. If you don't...'

'Matron Reed?' Flight Sergeant Parish called to her from his bed on the other side of the ward. 'I have a question for you and wondered if you could help put my thoughts straight about it.'

Matron swivelled on her heels and, leaving Evie to clean up the mess, headed over to find out what he wanted to ask her.

'I'll help,' Hazel said, coming over from where she'd been washing down bedside lockers. 'How does she always do that – turn up just when we wouldn't want her to?'

Evie shook her head. 'I don't know, but she does. Time and time again,' she whispered. She doubted Matron would hear over the cheerful chatter about Christmas arrangements at the hospital which Flight Sergeant Parish was engaging her in, but Evie dared not risk further annoying her boss. She was thankful Flight Sergeant Parish had called out to Matron when he did. It had saved Evie from a much longer telling off.

'What happened?' Hazel whispered, using a cloth to mop up the soapy water, wringing it out in the righted bucket.

'I don't know. I must have caught the handle with my arm,'

Evie said as she blotted up the spill with towels. 'It was an accident, that's all.'

Hazel sat back on her heels, giving Evie a searching look. 'Are you all right? Only you've been very quiet this morning. Not yourself at all.'

Evie wished she could tell her friend what had happened, but she couldn't for the time being because she knew what Hazel would say. That her answer to Ned should be yes! Hazel was well aware of how much Evie loved and admired Ned. But she didn't know the full story about her time married to Douglas and why Evie found the prospect of marrying again so abhorrent.

'I didn't sleep very well last night,' Evie admitted truthfully. In fact, she hadn't slept properly for the past three nights ever since Ned had proposed. 'I'm just tired.'

'You'd better try to get an early night tonight then,' Hazel advised.

Evie managed a small smile. 'I will.'

The spill was soon cleared up and Evie went to fetch another bucket of clean, hot soapy water to continue her work washing the bed frame. She was glad to see that Matron had left the ward by the time she got back. Putting the bucket down by the bed where she'd been working, she went over to speak to Flight Sergeant Parish for a moment.

'Thank you for stepping in like that. I appreciate it.' She gave him a rueful smile.

'I'm glad to help. Matron is far too hard on you nurses. It was some spilt soapy water, that's all. Nothing worth getting in trouble for. Anyway, it was interesting to hear what's planned for Christmas.'

'We try to make it as festive as we can, not just for all you patients but for us nurses who'll be on duty. I hope you'll enjoy it.'

'I'm sure I will. Now, as much as I hate to say it, don't let Matron come back and find you gossiping with me when you should be working.' He gave her a cheeky grin.

Evie laughed. 'Then I *would* be in trouble and probably sent packing to work in the sluice for the rest of the day. Thanks again for the distraction.'

'Happy to help any time.'

Returning to her work and taking extra care not to knock over the bucket, Evie forced her mind to concentrate on the job in hand. She had to put her worries to one side while she was at the hospital, hard though it was. Her personal problems would be resolved one way or the other. In the meantime, she had her chosen profession to concentrate on. It was her duty to be the best nurse for her patients.

CHAPTER 16

Evie usually enjoyed Hettie's shepherd's pie but tonight it seemed to have lost its flavour. She knew it wasn't the pie that was the problem – it was her. Nothing she ate would taste right, not with how her mind was in such a turmoil and after the awful day she'd had at the hospital getting into trouble with Matron. She would be glad when tomorrow came. Although the next day wasn't likely to be any better than this one. Ned's proposal would be hanging over her like a dark cloud until she worked out what she was going to do and did it.

For now, she knew she'd make poor company and was relieved that she'd been able to eat her evening meal on her own in the kitchen as the others were busy elsewhere in the house. As usual, Hettie had left Evie's plate of food ready for her in the range's warming oven, everyone else having eaten their meal earlier.

She had just finished the last mouthful of pie and put her knife and fork down on her empty plate, when the outside door opened and Thea came in, bringing a blast of chilly night air with her.

'Hello.' Thea greeted her. 'It's nippy out there tonight!' She shrugged off her coat, draping it over the back of a chair, then went to the range and held her hands over it to warm them. 'I've just been over at Reuben's. He was telling me about the plans for the Christmas carol concert at the hospital. Lady Campbell-Gryce has asked him to cut down a Christmas tree ready for the twenty-second.' Thea turned to face Evie. 'It sounds...' her words faltered. 'Are you all right?' She came over to the table, pulled out a chair and sat beside Evie.

'I'm...' Evie hesitated. She was going to say she was fine, but that wasn't true and if there was one person she knew who might give her good advice about what to do, and the emotional support she needed, it was Thea. She'd helped Evie in the past and might offer guidance with this problem as well.

Thea was peering at her with a look of concern. 'Evie?'

'I'm not all right,' Evie said, and dropped her gaze to her hands clasped in her lap. 'Ned proposed to me last Saturday.' She looked up to gauge her friend's reaction.

Thea was motionless for a few moments, her mouth a small 'o' shape. Finally, she said, 'I take it from your expression that it wasn't something you wanted to hear?'

Evie shook her head. 'Definitely not! Everything was fine, just as it was. I was very happy but now...' she waved a hand in the air in frustration. 'He's gone and spoilt it!'

'Have you given him an answer?'

'Not yet. I told him I needed to think about it. Although to be honest, my answer now is the same as it was immediately after he asked me. It's no, and will *always* be no, which is...' Evie's voice wavered, and Thea took hold of her hands in hers, giving them a gentle squeeze. 'I wish it could be otherwise, but I just *can't* do it again. Not after what I went through with

Douglas. I know Ned isn't like Douglas, not one little bit. But Douglas was nice too, until we were married and he became a bully and a tyrant. It was horrible, Thea! And I won't let it happen to me again.'

'I understand how you feel.' Thea's eyes were full of sympathy. 'You're not prepared to take a risk with Ned, even though it could work out well and you'd be happy together.'

'Because it could turn sour and my life would again be dominated by a man who was cruel and uncaring towards me. I misjudged before and I *promised* myself I would never put myself in that position ever again.'

Thea nodded. 'Marriage can be a blessing and a curse. I've seen it go both ways and, to be honest, it makes me inclined to agree with you after what you went through. From what I know of Ned, I don't think he would be an unkind husband, but I understand your reluctance to take a chance again.' She fell silent for a few moments, her expression thoughtful. 'There is another possibility, though. I've seen it work extremely well.'

'What's that?'

Thea looked her calmly in the eyes. 'That you *pretend* to be married.'

Evie stared at her friend in astonishment. 'Pretend? But people would quickly find out it wasn't true. You know what it's like around here with everyone knowing each other's business, well most of it – I've kept my history secret, thankfully. But if the village gossips got wind of it, they'd be quick to spread the news.'

'I appreciate that,' Thea agreed. 'Only don't dismiss the idea, because it's a genuine possibility. It would give you everything you would have if you were married, but without the legal bond. You would still be free to leave if things went wrong. One of my friends back in London fell in love with a man who was separated from his wife but she refused to give him a divorce. They knew they could never legally marry so instead they just pretended they were. And they're both happy together, with most people none the wiser.'

'But they live in London,' Evie countered, 'a huge city where it's easier to keep secrets and move to a new area where nobody would know them or have any reason to doubt their marriage. It's not the same here. Everyone would know that we hadn't got married at the church.'

'I agree it was easier for them in London, but I'm sure they aren't the only couple who appear to be husband and wife but aren't really married, even out here in the countryside. You and Ned could go away and supposedly marry while you're gone. Perhaps on a fictitious visit to see your mother? That would be plausible,' Thea said. 'Then you could come back here as a married couple and only you and Ned need to know the truth.'

'I couldn't live a lie like that when it came to my close friends. I'd want you to know, and Hettie and Flo too. You've all been so good to me. You're my family.'

'All right, I appreciate that, but apart from us three, no one else would know the truth. We'd all keep your secret. There's no doubt about that.' Thea's gaze held Evie's. 'You could trust us, you know. We all want you to be happy.'

Tears trickled down Evie's cheeks. Soundlessly, she put her head on Thea's shoulder and embraced her. 'Thank you,' she choked. And when she'd composed herself, 'Thank you, Thea,' she repeated softly. 'Thank you.'

Evie sat back and wiped her eyes with her fingers. 'You really surprised me there, Thea. It hadn't crossed my mind, the possibility of pretending we were married. I think I could accept that. We'd be married in all but the legal sense and I'd have the security of being able to walk away if things ever did go wrong.'

'What about Ned? Would he accept it?' Thea asked.

Evie thought about it. 'I just don't know. It all depends on his attitude to marriage. Whether he needs it to be a legal commitment in a church or registry office.' She let out a soft sigh, shaking her head. 'That's not a topic we've ever discussed. So I have no idea what he will think, but unless I can come up with another workable option, that's all I can offer him.'

'It's better than an outright 'no',' Thea said. She smiled. 'I hope it works out for you. I really do.'

'Thank you for listening and for your advice. If Ned won't agree to a pretend marriage, then I'm not sure there's anything left for us. It might be wiser to end our relationship and leave him free to find a woman who will marry him.'

'And how would you feel about that?' Thea asked gently.

Tears flooded into Evie's eyes and rolled down her cheeks once more. 'It would break my heart.'

Thea wrapped Evie in her arms and hugged her tightly. 'I hope it doesn't come to that. If Ned has any sense, he will understand and do what's necessary for you to be together in the only way you can.'

Evie nodded, unable to talk. She would speak to Ned about it as soon as possible. The uncertainty was hard to bear, so the sooner she knew where her future lay the better. Because if he didn't agree to a pretend marriage, then Evie wasn't sure she'd be able to cope with seeing him around or, even worse, stepping out with and eventually marrying someone else. She might have to leave and start again in a new hospital and a new home far from Rookery House. And that would break her heart even more.

CHAPTER 17

It was Thursday night and Flo was helping to set out the chairs ready for the singing group in the village hall. Positioning the three she'd carried over from the stacks at the side of the room, she felt a hand on her arm and turned to see Gloria standing beside her.

'I just wanted to say if you need to step out for a bit tonight, you do that,' Gloria said in a hushed voice. 'Do what's right for you.' She gave Flo an understanding look.

'I'm hoping I won't have to,' Flo replied, adjusting the angle of a chair so it fitted better into the semi-circle. 'I've been practising some carols, getting used to singing them again. I think I can do it. I *hope* I can sing, well, most of them.'

Gloria beamed at her. 'That's marvellous, ducks. I'm so pleased to 'ear that. They're such lovely songs to sing and it felt like a terrible shame for you not to be able to. But as I said, if you should need to step out at any point, it's fine by me.' She gave Flo's arm a gentle squeeze before letting go.

'Thank you, Gloria,' she told her friend, 'it helps having you looking out for me.'

Another member of the group came up to Gloria to ask her a question and Flo got on with fetching more chairs. She hoped she could stay to join in with the carols tonight. She wanted to. But realistically she knew that singing on her own with only Primrose or the chickens to hear her might prove much easier than singing along with the others. There was only one way to find out for sure and that was to try.

After leading the group through their vocal warm-ups, Gloria motioned with her hands for them to soften their voices, the notes growing fainter until they faded away into silence.

'Lovely!' Gloria gazed around the gathered women standing in a semi-circle in front of her, a delighted smile lighting up her face. 'I 'ave to say even just stretching our vocal cords to get them in tip-top condition ready to sing sounds marvellous tonight. But that ain't what they're expecting at the hospital next week, so we must move on to practising our carols for the first 'alf of this evening. You all know them so well, I ain't going to dwell on them. It's just a case of a quick polish to make them the best we can.'

Gloria glanced Flo's way and Flo nodded her encouragement.

'Okay, then. Let's start with *While Shepherds Watched their Flocks by Night*, and remember, no slipping into singing about them doing their laundry!' Gloria waggled her arched eyebrows theatrically.

'We used to get in trouble for singing about them washing their socks at school,' Hettie said. 'But some boys still did it. They couldn't help themselves.'

'I'll tell you what,' Gloria said, one hand on her hip, her eyes twinkling mischievously. 'In memory of those days, why don't we start with just the first verse and some sock washing, get it out of our systems?'

Flo and the rest of the women laughed.

'Ready Mrs P?' Gloria called over to Rosalind Platten who would accompany them on the piano at the carol concert and who worked at the hospital as quartermaster there.

'Whenever you are,' Rosalind confirmed and started to play the introduction.

'After four...' Gloria counted them in with beats of her hand. 'One... two... three... four...'

The women sang the familiar carol substituting *watched* for *washed* and *flocks* for *socks*, giggles breaking out as they sang. By the end of the four lines of the first verse, the village hall was ringing with laughter.

'Right,' Gloria called out after recovering her composure. 'Now let's do it for real. Make those words crisp and clear. Imagine yourself on that 'illside on Christmas Eve, feel the words and... enjoy!' She looked to Rosalind, who once again played the introduction, and Gloria counted them in.

As she sang, Flo pictured a starlit night where shepherds sat around a fire guarding their sheep, while up above an extra bright star shone out. She relaxed into the song and they were halfway through before it dawned on her that she was actually singing a carol with the others. She was doing it! The realisation made her falter for a split second, but she didn't let it stop her. She loved the way the song sounded with the swell of different voices. It told of so many Christmases past, not just hers, but spanning back generations. Times when people gathered to sing together in homes, schools, churches or out carolling in the streets. It warmed her heart to be singing it again.

As the last note faded and the hall fell silent, Flo let out a sigh of pleasure. She'd done it. Gloria caught her eye and raised a questioning eyebrow. Flo gave her a happy smile and Gloria returned it.

'Excellent!' Gloria clapped her hands and surveyed the group of women. 'What a delightful sound.'

'Picturing those shepherds on the 'illside 'elped,' Edith called out. 'I ain't never thought of it like that before.'

'Sometimes we forget, but carols are a sort of storytelling,' said Gloria. 'The words ain't just to make a delightful sound but to remember that night of long ago. Our next carol is *Silent Night*. This time imagine that peaceful stable with the newborn babe, the dark sky overhead, the shepherds and angels. The *wonder* of it all!'

Flo sang along with all the other women, growing in confidence and surety of her voice as they sang carol after carol. But the final one tripped her up. The moment Gloria announced they would be ending the concert with *The Holly and the Ivy*, Flo knew she had to get out of there. That was the one carol she could not sing.

Gloria must have read her reaction because instead of looking to Rosalind to begin playing, she glanced at her watch and said, 'Time's running out fast on us tonight. Flo, would you mind nipping into the kitchen and getting the kettle on and the tea things set out while we practise this last one? It'll save us some time.'

'Of course.' Flo sent a message of thanks to Gloria with her eyes before leaving the hall.

She made it to the safety of the kitchen and stood leaning against the table as the singing began again, her head bowed and her heart hammering inside her. Taking some steadying breaths, her pulse slowed, and she started preparing for the tea break, filling up the kettle at the sink and putting it on to boil, then taking out the teacups and setting them out on the trolley. All the while the words and tune of *The Holly and the Ivy* filtered through from the hall, and Flo realised that the song's effect on her had diminished a little compared with when she'd heard it sung the previous week. It still brought back the memory of that terrible night, but she found herself appreciating its beautiful melody, and the way her friends were singing it. Flo knew she was a long way off singing it again herself, but she had perhaps taken a step forwards if she was beginning to enjoy hearing it.

When Gloria came into the kitchen a few minutes later, Flo had everything ready for the tea break. She had poured boiling water into the big teapot and she'd set the biscuits that Hettie had made out on a plate.

'Thanks for doing this,' Gloria said. 'We're all parched and ready for a brew before we start again.' She came over to Flo and put her arm around her, lowering her voice. 'You all right, ducks?'

Flo nodded. 'I just couldn't manage the last one.'

'No problem. You sang the others beautifully. I'm 'oping you'll be up to joining us at the carol concert – only singing what feels right for you, though. If you keep in the back row, you can slip away if you feel the need.'

'I'd like to be there with you all. Standing at the back sounds like a good idea in case I get to a bit I can't do. I know for sure that I can't sing *The...*' Flo hesitated, not sure she could even say the name of what had been her favourite carol since childhood. She lifted her chin. '*The Holly and the Ivy,*' she said with determination. 'It's just too...' She waved her hand in place of words.

'As I said, it ain't a problem. You know 'ow you feel and you must do the right thing for you.' Gloria gave her a squeeze before letting her go. 'Now let's get the tea in there before we 'ave a riot of thirsty singers on our 'ands!'

CHAPTER 18

Evie couldn't wait any longer to speak to Ned, so rather than going to the nurses' sitting room for her afternoon break, she put on her scarf, coat and gloves in the cloakroom and went outside to find him. It would be a week tomorrow that he'd proposed and since then she'd spent a lot of time thinking about the best thing to do. She had passed many hours lying awake in the night, worrying. After talking to Thea a couple of days ago, Evie was certain she had made the right decision and just needed to tell Ned her answer, though finding a chance for them to be alone together around their work commitments had proven hard and she still hadn't had the opportunity to speak to him. But after another night with far too little sleep, Evie couldn't wait any more – she would locate Ned and tell him this afternoon.

It was cold outside but at least the low winter sun was shining weakly and the pale blue sky was more cheering than the heavy grey clouds that had persisted over the past few days. Making her way into the walled garden, Evie spotted

Ned over by the perimeter wall, half-way up a ladder from where he was working on the espaliered fruit trees. And importantly, he was alone.

With her heart pounding at the thought of what she was about to tell him, Evie made her way towards him along the pathways between the vegetable beds. Climbing down from the ladder propped up against the wall, Ned saw her and waved.

'What brings you out here this afternoon? Not that I'm not pleased to see you,' he said as she drew near, before leaning in and kissing her cheek. 'If it's Mr White you're looking for on a job for Matron, then you'll find him in the glasshouse.' She thought he sounded different, as if he was forcing himself to be light-hearted.

Evie glanced over to the large greenhouse that was built onto the brick wall close to the bothy, where Evie could see the head gardener busy at work. She wished she *had* come to see Mr White with a message – anything but this.

'It's you I've come to see. I'm on my afternoon break. What are you working on?' she asked, wanting to preserve their good terms for a little while longer because she feared that what she was about to tell him would likely end their relationship.

'I'm checking the ties between the branches and the wires and adding new ones in some places.' Ned gestured towards the nearest apple tree, its branches trained horizontally outwards along the wall over long years by gardeners restraining and shaping it. It was so different from the free growing fruit trees in the orchard at Rookery House. There the trees were left largely to their own accord, responding only to nature – the growing conditions, sun, wind and rain – with only some occasional essential pruning to keep them healthy and growing. In comparison, Evie thought, the espaliered trees appeared trapped and controlled, and all of a sudden she was thinking of her marriage, how Douglas's behaviour, wants and rules had restrained her, shaping her life in a way that was unnatural to her.

'Evie?' Ned's voice broke into her thoughts.

She attempted a smile but it never came. 'I need to talk to you about what you asked me last Saturday.'

'Yes,' he said simply, and she saw the look of sadness deep in his eyes.

'I've come to give you my answer.'

'I thought so.'

Ned calmly regarded her, and she knew that he must have been thinking about this quite as much as she had. Shared her sleepless nights, her agony. Of course he must. Her heart went out to the man she loved, and it almost broke her to hear herself speak the words she'd rehearsed over and over but never wanted to say.

'I'm… I'm afraid my answer is no. It has to be no.' Evie watched the colour drain from his face. 'But please understand, it's not because I don't want to marry you, it's because *I can't*.'

Ned frowned. 'I don't understand. Is there somebody else? Or is it because of what happened with Douglas?'

'There isn't anybody else but you, of course not!' It hadn't crossed her mind he'd think that a possibility. 'But yes, it's about Douglas. I simply can't marry again because of how things became when I married him. It's not because I don't love you, because I do, very much. And I wish with all my heart I could give you the answer you want, but I can't.' She paused for a moment before adding quietly, 'There is another way we could be together.'

'What do you mean?'

She saw a flicker of hope in his eyes, and so she just went ahead and said it. 'We could pretend to be married.'

For a few silent moments, he simply stared at her, a stunned expression on his face. 'But how could that work?'

'We would go away, visit my mother and come back saying we'd got a special licence, then married while we were staying with her. No one would be any the wiser and we could live together as husband and wife.'

Ned shook his head. 'But I don't want that. I want to be your husband. Your lawful husband.'

It was as Evie had feared. She felt as if a stone had settled in the pit of her stomach. She was sure this was the beginning of the end for them.

'Do people really pretend to be married?' he asked.

'Some friends of Thea's in London couldn't get married because the man's wife wouldn't give him a divorce, so they pretended they were and are still very happy together.'

'But that's in London, where it's easier for people to keep secrets. Here in Great Plumstead … I just don't think it would ever work.'

'I know it would be difficult and unusual and not what you were hoping for, but that's all I can offer you, Ned. I'm sorry.' She turned to go.

'Evie.' Ned took hold of her hand gently. 'I'm not like Douglas. I promise I would never hurt you. I swear on my life.' His beseeching eyes held hers.

'I know you're not like him, otherwise I'd never have stepped out with you in the first place, but even so, I still can't marry you or anyone ever again.' Evie's voice wavered as she blinked back tears. 'I'm sorry Ned. I do love you, if that's any consolation.'

She squeezed his hand and then walked away, resisting the urge to look back because she'd given him her answer and now she had to let him have time to think. Was it the end, or could they return to how they'd been before? Or would Ned come around to the idea of pretending they were married? Evie didn't know. All she knew for sure was she would have to accept his decision and the consequences it would mean for her.

CHAPTER 19

Thea always enjoyed spending Saturday afternoons with the children. After a busy week's work, it was good to do other things. This afternoon she and Flo were taking George, Betty and Emily for a walk in the nearby wood. They were strolling down the lane from Rookery House, when Thea spotted a familiar figure bicycling towards them from the direction of Great Plumstead Hall.

'Ned!' the children chorused as he reached them and came to a halt, dismounting from his bicycle.

'How are you, Ned?' Flo greeted him, and he nodded briefly in return.

'We're going *exploring* – do you want to come?' George asked.

'Not today,' Ned said, giving the little boy a smile. 'But thanks for the offer. I was hoping I could speak to you, Thea.' He looked to her, his expression now serious.

She guessed what he wanted to talk to her about. Evie had told Thea she'd given Ned her answer, along with the suggestion that they pretend to be married, and that it hadn't gone down well.

'Of course. Flo, would you take the children into the wood and I'll catch up with you in a bit?' Thea suggested, thinking it best that whatever Ned had to say was said without the others listening.

'Of course, we'll see you in there. Come on you lot, let's go and see what we can find.' Flo gave Thea an understanding look and then shepherded the children towards the nearby entrance of the wood.

Once they were out of earshot, Thea asked, 'What do you want to talk to me about?'

'You can probably guess,' he replied.

'Maybe, but I'd rather you tell me than assume what I know already, in case I'm mistaken.'

Ned took a steadying breath. 'Last Saturday I proposed to Evie and she said that she needed time to think about it, which was fair enough as I'd sprung it on her. Yesterday she told me she can't marry me, or anyone, and instead she suggested that we could *pretend* to be married.' He frowned. 'But I don't want that. The reason I asked her is that I want to be officially married to her. To publicly declare my love and commitment to her.'

'That's not something Evie feels she can do,' Thea pointed out. 'However, she could do the other option. I know it's not the same, without a ceremony either in a church or registry office, but that's only a small part of being married. A marriage is much more about the days, months and years that come after that wedding day, isn't it?'

'In theory, I suppose,' Ned agreed. 'But it also shows a couple are committed to each other. They make vows to each other that last the rest of their lives together.'

'From my experience, a couple might make vows and

legally bind themselves during the marriage ceremony, but it doesn't necessarily mean that they are fully committed… That they will *always* love and care for each other. Sadly, I know of too many marriages where that hasn't proved to be the case and where being married makes one or both parties miserable, or one lives in fear of what their husband or wife might to do them,' Thea said. 'Evie's marriage to Douglas was legal and made in a church but look how that turned out. How terribly he treated her. It's no wonder that she feels she can't ever marry again.'

'*I'm* not like Douglas!' Ned said. 'I'd never hurt her.'

'But she never thought Douglas would either. If it's any help, *I* don't think you would ever hurt Evie. However, you must remember that she was so badly treated before and it's left her with a deep and painful wound.' Thea reached out and touched Ned's arm. 'I've seen how well a couple pretending they're married can work out. How happy they can be. I think you and Evie could have a very happy life together too, if you gave it a chance.'

'But it's not the normal thing to do!'

Thea let out a laugh. 'Would you rather be normal or happy?'

Ned looked uncomfortable.

'You have a choice of accepting what Evie can do and being together for the rest of your lives – you could live like any other married couple except for a few minutes' legal ceremony. Or you can refuse because it's not what most people do, and risk losing Evie forever. I think there's a good chance that she may move away from here because it would be too hard for her to stay. So, the question is, which do you value more? Evie's love and a life together or insisting it can only happen if you're legally married?' Thea's eyes met his and she held his gaze before he looked away.

'I don't know,' Ned said softly, shaking his head. 'I need to think about it. I love Evie with all my heart... but I want her to be my wife.'

'Then you have a lot of thinking and soul-searching to do. I hope for your sake and Evie's that you make the right decision and not one that you will regret for the rest of your life.'

'What would you do in my position?' Ned asked her directly.

'I think you already know the answer to that question. You just need to find an answer of your own.' Thea gave him a sympathetic smile. 'Now I must catch up with Flo and the children. I wish you well, Ned, I really do. If you decide to be together, you will have my complete support and total discretion.'

'Thank you.'

Leaving him standing in the road, Thea took the path into the wood. She desperately hoped that Ned would make the right decision. That he'd step outside the conventions of what was normal and take the chance that could lead to him and Evie having a lifetime of happiness together.

CHAPTER 20

There was a murmur of anticipation in the packed church this afternoon as the congregation waited for the children to arrive from the school. Thea was sitting in a pew three rows from the front, along with Hettie, Ted and Flo. Marianne, Emily and baby Bea sat in the row behind them alongside Prue and Nancy.

'The children must have been spotted,' Thea said, turning to Emily and looking down the church past her. 'How exciting!'

Emily clapped her hands and twisted around to look too.

With only two more days to go until Christmas Day, coming here to watch the nativity play felt like the perfect way to start the festive season. Thea only wished that George and Betty's mother, Jess, could be here to watch it too, but she couldn't get up from London until Christmas Eve because of her job sewing uniforms in one of the garment factories in the East End.

'Here they come!' Hettie said, standing up to see.

Thea watched the Headmaster of the school lead a

procession up the aisle. The pairs of children walking behind him were already dressed in readiness for their performance; angels, shepherds and the Three Kings came marching in. She saw George and Betty go past her and the sight of them proudly wearing their costumes brought a lump to Thea's throat.

'Look! Do you recognise that purple cloak?' Hettie asked Ted in a barely contained whisper, pointing to the little boy playing one of the kings. 'I'm sure it's the one Sidney wore for the same part, what must have been sixty years ago or there abouts! How lovely!'

'It looks the same,' Ted agreed. 'I remember how much Sid liked the colour of it.'

They watched as the children were settled at the front, and then the Reverend Balding stepped forward.

'Good afternoon, everyone, and welcome to our special nativity service.'

Thea might have seen these services before, but they never failed to move her. There was something so touching about children acting out the age-old story. It was a performance played out in schools and churches across the country, linking people together in the here and now, as well as harking back to the story of the first Christmas through all the generations that came between. Thea was engrossed as the children, many of whom she knew, performed their roles with the joy of Christmas on their faces, accompanied at intervals with the congregation singing carols.

The final bars of *While Shepherds Watched their Flocks by Night* had ended and Thea had just sat down in the pew again when she saw Miss Walters, the infant teacher, beckoning the four boys playing shepherds to stand up ready to play their part and approach the imaginary stable area at the front of the church. Thea's heart filled with pride, the same as any mother's would, as she watched George make his way to the stable, wearing a long tunic, striped headdress and carrying a crook in his hand. He didn't have any words to say, but from the earnest expression on his face, he was giving his all to the role. Once the shepherds were seated near the manger with Mary, Joseph and baby Jesus, it was the time for another carol.

'Please turn to page one hundred and twelve for *Hark the Herald Angels Sing*,' the Reverand Balding announced before the pipes of the organ blasted out the introductory bars.

The congregation rose and Thea joined in. She wasn't a regular church goer like Hettie, but she always enjoyed coming along at Christmas and singing the carols. The words and music she'd first learned as a child were part of Christmas and she loved to sing them. And so did Flo, Thea thought, glancing at her friend who stood on her left and whose beautiful voice was soaring, clear and pitch perfect. Flo must have sensed Thea looking at her as she turned and gave her a smile as she sang.

This time, rather than waiting until the end of the carol, Miss Walters guided the children playing the angels to arrive during the singing. They moved into position to stand behind the stable area, their arms spread wide in their white gowns, as if pronouncing the glory. Thea could tell that Betty was fit to bursting with delight as she acted out her role, which she'd practised over and over at home, desperate to get it right. Thea's heart swelled watching her and she felt hugely grateful to have Betty and George in her life.

'There's something about a nativity, it always...' Hettie said, pulling a clean handkerchief out of her handbag as they sat down in the pews once more, after the last verse. She dabbed at her eyes. 'Having our two in it makes it even more... It's a lovely thing, but it gets to me in here.' She put her hand to her chest.

Thea gave her friend a sympathetic smile. 'They've done so well, too. Just look at them,' she said in a hushed voice nodding her head towards where George and Betty were both intently watching the Three Kings who'd just arrived bearing their gifts of gold, frankincense and myrrh which they were presenting to the baby Jesus.

Hettie sniffed and dabbed at her eyes again with her handkerchief. Thea noticed her friend didn't refuse when Ted, who was sitting next to Hettie, offered her his hand to hold.

CHAPTER 21

Gathered with the other members of the village singing group outside the front door of Great Plumstead Hall Hospital, Flo listened as Gloria gave them final words of advice.

'The most important thing is to *enjoy* yourselves. Let the songs fill you up with joy, picture the story you're telling and *smile*,' Gloria encouraged them, her bright-red lipsticked lips curving upwards. 'I'm so proud of you all and it fills my 'eart to sing with you, be it 'ere or on our nights at the village 'all. So come on ladies, let's bring some Christmas spirit to the patients and staff.'

Despite Gloria's rousing words, Flo's stomach was still knotting with unease and she hung back as the other women went in through the door. The feeling had been growing all day and she wasn't sure if she could perform now that they were here. She might have sung at Thursday practice in the village hall and earlier today in church during the nativity, but they were different: she hadn't had to stand in front of an audience. This was going to feel exposed and was stirring up memories of the last time she had planned to go carol singing with her friends from work back in Manchester. Only it had never happened because enemy bombers attacked the city.

'Flo?' Gloria's voice broke into her thoughts. 'You all right, ducks?'

She gave a small shake of her head. 'I'm nervous, I don't know...' she admitted.

'That's to be expected,' Gloria reassured her. 'Remember what I told you? Do what you can and if you feel you need to step away, then do.' She put her arm through Flo's. 'Let's go indoors out of the cold.'

Flo allowed herself to be led inside and the sight of the magnificent Christmas tree which almost reached the ceiling of the hall made her gasp. It was beautiful. Coloured baubles dangling from its branches twisted gently in the moving air, reflecting diamonds of light from the burning candles.

'The cloakroom's this way.' Mrs Platten beckoned them to follow her.

As they walked through the hallway, Flo caught glimpses of the wards through open doors. She'd heard a lot about the hospital from Evie but this was the first time Flo had been here herself. It was strange to see a hospital set up in a grand house, the functional unexpectedly blended with the grandeur.

After leaving her coat, hat, scarf and gloves in the cloakroom with those of the rest of the singing group, Flo followed the others back into the hall where Lady Campbell-Gryce was waiting for them.

'Welcome everyone!' She greeted them with a beaming smile. 'We're so delighted to have you here this evening and we are all looking forward to hearing your beautiful singing. But first I thought it would be wonderful for our lovely patients to meet you all as I'm sure they tire of the same old faces. So please,' she gestured with her hand towards the wards and the Recreation Room, 'do introduce yourselves.'

Flo didn't know whether to be relieved or disappointed that their performance wouldn't happen straight away as she'd expected. On the one hand, it delayed the challenge for a bit, but on the other she wanted it over and done with. However, that was out of her hands following her Ladyship's request. She'd just have to get on with it.

Flo headed for the nearest ward, which according to the name plate on the door was Dining Room Ward and was where the family had once eaten their meals. Only now, Flo thought, stepping through the doorway, what she imagined must have been a grand dining table had been replaced by white metal-framed hospital beds and lockers. She took in the large floor-to-ceiling windows, the huge marble mantlepiece and the intricately decorated ceiling, which was far more impressive than in any house she'd ever lived in. At home with her family, meals had been eaten at the kitchen table as there'd been no dining room. Even at Rookery House where there was one, it was used for Marianne's dressmaking or for visitors to sleep in, meals were eaten at the table in the kitchen.

'It's fancy in here, isn't it?!' a voice said from close by.

Flo turned around to see a man sitting in a wheelchair. She noticed one of his pyjama legs, showing beneath his dressing gown, was pinned up where his lower leg was missing.

'Very,' she agreed. 'I'm not used to being in a place like this.'

'Me neither. It was quite a contrast after the hospital in Norwich. Are you one of the singers come to entertain us?' he asked.

'Yes.' Flo stepped nearer to him so they could hear each other as the level of noise in the ward had gone up with other members of the group chatting to patients. A roar of laughter came from Gloria who was talking to a patient at the far end of the ward.

'You lot have cheered the place up and you haven't even started singing yet,' the man commented drily, his brown eyes full of amusement. 'I'm John Parish.' He held out his hand for her to shake.

'Flo Butterworth,' Flo said, shaking it.

'You're from Lancashire... going by your accent?'

'That's right, from Lancaster. Born and raised there until I was fourteen, then my family moved to Manchester for my dad's job. What about you – where are you from? Yorkshire, if I'm not mistaken?'

He laughed. 'You're not. I'm from God's own country. What's brought you here to Norfolk, then?'

Flo pulled up a nearby chair and sat down so that she could speak to him properly facing each other, rather than having to look down at him sitting in the wheelchair. 'I'm a Land Girl and work at Rookery House here in the village. Evie Jones, one of your nurses, lives there too.'

'Ah! Nurse Jones is a wonderful nurse. Very kind and patient with us all.'

'She's a wonderful friend, too.'

'What made you decide to be a Land Girl? It's not an easy job, hard physical work and outside in all weathers. We used to see them working in the fields near the aerodrome I was at.'

'The simple answer is because I love growing things. I joined the Land Army and trained for market gardening rather than general farm work with animals,' Flo explained. 'Although at Rookery House we have got a house cow, pigs, chickens and rabbits, which I help look after too, but most of my work is growing fruit and vegetables. I love what I do.'

'Then you are fortunate. Loving your work makes a big difference.'

'What about you?' Flo asked. 'Which service are you in?'

'The RAF. I'm a...' he hesitated. 'I *was* a flight engineer on a Lancaster bomber. But my days of doing that are over.' He glanced down at where his right foot should be. 'I'll be medically discharged once I'm fit enough to go home.'

'I'm sorry that's happened to you,' Flo said. 'It must be hard.'

John was silent for a few moments before replying, 'Not as hard as for the rest of my crew who didn't make it.' He stared off into the distance for a moment before returning his gaze to Flo. 'I'm lucky to still be here – well, most of me.' He gave a shrug of a shoulder. 'I miss my fellow crew members every single day. We were like brothers, but we all knew that each time we got in that plane we might not come back. So we vowed that if it happened and some of us bought it, then the others would carry on, live well for them. Life is precious and fragile. We need to cherish it if we're lucky enough to still have it.'

Flo's eyes filled with tears. 'I lost my family in the Manchester Christmas Blitz,' she said, just loud enough for him to hear, the words tumbling out before she could stop them. 'I understand what it's like to suddenly lose those you're close to.'

John put his hand on her arm. 'It's hard. But you are carrying on now, doing work you love. Your family would be proud of you.'

She blinked away her tears. 'I didn't think I'd be able to come here today for the carol singing because of what happened.' She told him about the night of the bombing and how she hadn't been able to sing carols since then until the singing group had been asked to perform here and had started rehearsing. 'I've practised, but now it's come to it, I'm not sure if I can do it or not.'

'What do you think might happen if you try?' he asked, and for a moment Flo was knocked off guard by his directness.

She considered his question. 'That I can't sing the words. That they just won't come out.'

'Did that happen in rehearsals?'

'No.'

He gave her an enquiring look.

'Or I might crumple and cry,' Flo suggested, trying to make light of it but failing to raise her spirits at all. 'Or just make a fool of myself.'

He raised an eyebrow. 'Have either of those things happened, when people heard you sing?'

'No,' she told him, her mind arcing back to when Reuben had heard her, and Bess – and the rooks!

'It sounds to me, speaking as an engineer here, that the vocal mechanics are all in good working order. So, what else might be stopping you?' His eyes met hers for a few seconds before she had to look away, staring down at the floor.

She heard herself say, 'The feeling that by singing carols and on today of all days, on the anniversary of their death, I would be betraying my family.'

Flo covered her face with her hands. She'd finally admitted to herself how deeply she still felt the sudden loss of her family. How much the wounds had not healed. For a moment she was back in Manchester that night, minutes before the bomb fell, standing by the kitchen sink. Then she was by her family's graves again, silently and futilely wishing her loved ones weren't gone.

A voice brought her back to the here and now, to the smell of carbolic soap and the rich sound of Gloria's bellowing laughter. Somebody was speaking to her. John, the injured airman.

'It's understandable how you link singing carols with

losing your family,' he said gently. 'You won't ever forget what happened … but singing carols isn't betraying your family. They would want you to be happy and to enjoy life.'

Flo lowered her hands and folded her arms tightly about her body. 'I'm not sure I can enjoy it,' she told him. 'It's easier said than done.'

'I agree. But worth a go, don't you think?' His face was earnest. 'I hope you'll join in and sing some of the carols today.'

'That's what Gloria said. She's our singing group leader.' Flo glanced to where Gloria was holding court, telling some tale about her time when she used to be a singer in London before she got married. Her bright fuchsia-pink dress stood out against the metal-framed beds with their starched white sheets and pale blue blankets.

'She looks quite a character,' John said.

'She is, and the loveliest person, too,' Flo agreed.

Lady Campbell-Gryce appeared in the doorway of the ward and clapped her hands. 'Ladies, if you'd like to take your places in the hallway and staff, if you can assist our patients into the hall, please, we are ready for the concert to begin.'

'It's time.' John's eyes met Flo's. 'Go out there and sing in honour of your family, because I think they'd want you to keep singing and not stop. Sing for them. And I'll listen and enjoy every second of it in honour of my fallen friends, of my crew who didn't make it and can't sit here with me.'

Flo saw the tears well up in John's eyes and she swallowed painfully, her throat thick with emotion. Then she lifted her chin and told him, 'I'll do my best, John.'

Standing in the back row of the singers, Flo's heart was pounding inside her chest. She breathed slowly and deeply, fixing her gaze on the Christmas tree and doing her best to blot out the sea of faces waiting for them to start. There were mobile patients standing and others in wheelchairs, like John Parish, who'd been wheeled into the hall to watch. She'd also seen a couple of patients whose hospital beds had been moved over to the open doorways of the wards so they wouldn't miss out on the concert.

'Ready ladies?' Gloria's voice rang out loud and clear. 'We'll start with *O Come All Ye Faithful*.' She turned to Mrs Platten, who was seated at the piano to the side of the hall. The older woman gave a nod in response and then played the introduction.

Flo focused her attention on Gloria, who counted them in with beats of her hand and as one they began to sing. The first few lines of the carol felt wobbly in Flo's throat and they came out much quieter than usual. But they were there and she was singing in front of the audience. Spurred on by that and the uplifting feeling that she always got from singing with the group, everybody's voices coming together to make a rich and varied sound, Flo kept on going. Note by note, word by word, she gradually sang more strongly, her confidence in her ability to do it growing.

By the time Gloria had guided them through two more carols, Flo dared to glance around at the audience and spotted Evie who gave her an encouraging smile, which Flo returned.

More carols followed and Flo felt herself relax, the tension dropping from her shoulders and the tightness in her throat melting away.

Gloria announced that the next song would be *The Holly and the Ivy* – and panic flared in Flo, her pulse racing. She needed to go, slip away into the background, get out of there as fast as she could. She frantically scanned the hallway for its nearest exit – and her focus landed on John Parish, sat in his wheelchair.

The injured airman, the only one of his crew to survive, was giving her a double thumbs-up signal and a calm look of confidence. He believed she could do it. Someone who until a short while ago she'd never met. And yet they had shared their stories with each other. He hadn't given up. He'd lost his friends and part of his leg, but he hadn't lost his spirit, or the will to live on.

As Mrs Platten played the introduction and Gloria counted them in, Flo took a deep breath, closed her eyes and began to sing. The words were wobbly to start with but they quickly became stronger and clearer. It was the carol she'd loved so much, her favourite since childhood and the one she spent all year looking forward to. She sang like the girl she'd been, with her family around her, and she sang *for* her family, her voice soaring like a bird set free.

Flo was so deeply absorbed in the song that she didn't realise the other voices had fallen away until she was halfway through the second verse. She snapped her eyes open and saw Gloria watching her, her mouth open in astonishment; Gloria gestured for Flo to keep singing.

For an instant, Flo hesitated, but then knowing that she *could* carry on now, she sang on with her solo. Gloria brought the other women in to join with the chorus, but Flo sang the rest of the verses alone. Her clear, powerful voice filled the hallway with its pine-scented tree, sprigs of red-berried holly, garlands of ivy and vases of Christmas roses. As she came to the end of the last verse a burst of applause broke out and she noticed Gloria mopping her eyes with a handkerchief. She'd done it and it felt wonderful, it was like a spell had been lifted.

Glancing over to John, she saw he was clapping

enthusiastically and beaming, his cheeks shiny with tears. She mouthed the words 'Thank you' to him.

Gloria addressed their audience. 'Now please do join us singing this last carol. Its message is one we send to you all, this Christmas and always.'

As Flo sang the final song, *We Wish You a Merry Christmas*, along with many of the audience, she realised that a weight seemed to have lifted from her, and she looked forward to this year's Christmas in a way she hadn't since her family had passed. She would always miss them, and think of them every day, but she could and should still make her life one filled with joy. That was the way to honour them and keep her memory of them.

As John had reminded her, life was precious and fragile and those who were lucky to still have it should live it well.

CHAPTER 22

As the last words and music of *We Wish You a Merry Christmas* faded away, the patients and staff watching the carol concert burst into enthusiastic applause and cheers of appreciation. Evie joined in eagerly. She'd loved listening to the wonderful performance in this beautiful, pine-scented space that was lit by flickering candles which bathed everyone's faces in a soft light and cast moving reflections off the glass baubles and other decorations hanging from the Christmas tree. It was a delight for her senses and so evocative of the festive season. Today's event had been a huge success.

Evie caught Flo's attention and waved, sending her a look of congratulations. She knew how difficult Flo had found it to try singing carols once more; her friend had pushed herself to overcome her fear. Through her sheer grit and determination, Flo had freed herself and even been able to sing a surprise solo of the carol she'd believed it would be impossible for her to sing ever again. Evie was so proud of her friend; listening to her solo verses of *The Holly and the Ivy* had warmed her heart.

She looked forward to giving Flo the hugest of hugs, but

first Evie was determined to catch up with Ned. She'd spotted him standing on the opposite side of the hall, near to the head gardener Mr White and his wife, whom Ned lodged with. It was the first time Evie had seen Ned since she'd given him her answer four days ago. She still didn't know what he was going to do, whether he would agree to her proposition or not. He could have come to find her at the hospital but hadn't, and Evie suspected that he was avoiding her.

Ned had spoken to Thea about Evie's refusal to marry him – Thea had told Evie as soon as she'd returned from her shift. But other than that, she did not know what he was thinking or if he'd come to a final decision of his own. She knew she had to give him time, but the waiting and not knowing was hard and now she had the chance to speak to him, to see if he would give her at least some sign of what he was thinking, if not an outright answer.

Making her way slowly through the throng of people in the hall, singers, staff members and patients happily intermingling, Evie headed to where Ned had been, but by the time she arrived there was no sign of him, only Mr White and his wife, munching on mince pies.

'Do you know where Ned is?' Evie asked.

'He was here a moment ago.' Mr White glanced to his left and right. 'He can't be far away. I'll tell him you're looking for him, shall I?'

'Yes, please. I...' She was interrupted by the arrival of Matron Reed.

'Nurse Jones, can you see to Flight Sergeant Parish, make sure he gets back to his bed safely?'

'Yes Matron,' Evie agreed, hoping that Mr White would see Ned and that he'd come and find her. In the meantime, she had work to attend to and made her way over to where Flight

Sergeant Parish was sitting at the side of the hall in his wheelchair.

'What did you think of our little Christmas Concert?' Evie asked.

'It was smashing. Sent shivers along my spine listening to the singing and that solo was amazing...'

Evie followed the path of his gaze and saw Flo, who was amongst a group of singers being spoken to by Lady Campbell-Gryce. Evie beckoned for Flo to come over and, waiting until her Ladyship had moved on to speak to somebody else, Flo joined them.

'You said you didn't think you could do it, and *then* look what you did!' Flight Sergeant Parish held out his hand to Flo and she took hold of it. 'You were fantastic. When I said you should try, I didn't think you'd end up singing it all by yourself! But there you go, some people are born show-offs...'

Evie was amazed to see the look that passed between her friend and Flight Sergeant Parish. It was as if they were old friends, easy in each other's company.

'I'm joking of course.' Flight Sergeant Parish winked. 'I'm so glad you sang solo – it was beautiful.'

'It was amazing!' Evie added. 'I am so proud of you, Flo. I know that can't have been easy, but you did it anyway.'

Flo's cheeks had grown pink. 'The funny thing is I didn't think about it – I just did it! When the others' voices faded away, I was so deeply absorbed in singing it, that I didn't even realise.'

'It proved beyond a doubt that you can do it.' Flight Sergeant Parish squeezed Flo's hand. 'Your family would be so happy for you.'

Flo nodded. 'Thank you for what you said earlier.' And to Evie she said, 'I was given a highly effective pep-talk and it helped a lot.'

'Good,' said Evie. 'And I'm so pleased you two have become friends.'

'I'm glad I could help.' Flight Sergeant Parish explained to Evie, 'When you go through something like we all have, it changes things, but you must make sure it doesn't change everything for the worse. That you still hang on to the things that are dear to you for both yourself and those you remember.' He fell silent for a moment before giving Evie a wide smile. 'I wouldn't say no to a mince pie if you can get me one, please! I dare not venture into the crowd in this wheelchair for fear of running someone over.'

'Of course.' Evie touched his shoulder. 'Flo, would you like a mince pie, too?'

'Yes please,' Flo said. 'I'm hungry now. I was so nervous before the concert that I couldn't eat a thing.'

Leaving Flo and Flight Sergeant Parish chatting, Evie made her way over to the refreshments table. She'd seen them talking earlier and was glad that he'd been able to help Flo. He was a good character to have on the ward and she would miss him when he was discharged. But at least he'd be going home – there'd be no more fighting for him. In the meantime, they had the festive season to celebrate here at the hospital and the carol concert had just got it off to a splendid start.

She only hoped it wouldn't be too much longer until she talked to Ned.

CHAPTER 23

Christmas Day

'We were so pleased to hear how you sang at the concert.' Flo's gran's voice came down the telephone line all the way from Lancaster.

Her grandad added, 'The patients must have appreciated it, what with being in hospital at Christmas.'

Flo pictured the pair of them huddled together in the red telephone box at the end of the next street from theirs, holding the receiver between them so they could both hear what she said and speak to her. She'd written and told them about the concert and her fears about singing in it and why.

'We're proud of you,' her gran said.

'Thank you. It wasn't easy but sometimes you just have to push yourself and then you're glad you did.' Flo cradled the receiver against her ear wishing that she could see her grandparents today but at least talking to them on the telephone, from her perch on the bottom of the stairs at Rookery House, was some immediate contact and better than letters.

'Are you having a lovely day?' she asked.

'Aye,' her grandad said, sounding impressed, 'we had a lovely dinner with plenty of veg from the allotment to go with the meat. Thought we might wander by the plot on our way home before it gets dark.'

'Even on Christmas Day, he can't keep away from the place!' her gran said good-naturedly. 'I've come prepared with a flask of tea. I know what he's like.'

Flo laughed. Her grandparents were such a close couple, knowing and understanding what was important to each other. Her gran appreciated how much the allotment meant to her grandad, and rather than moan about him going there even on Christmas Day, she would go with him, and they'd share a hot drink either sitting on the bench outside or inside the shed if it was raining.

'Enjoy it, it's a special place,' Flo told them.

They chatted for a little longer until her grandparents' money ran out and they said hurried goodbyes.

Putting the receiver back in its cradle, Flo smiled to herself, her heart warm and full after speaking to her grandparents. Until she'd moved to Manchester with her parents, brother and sister, they'd always spent Christmas with her grandparents. Now so much had changed. It was just her and her gran and grandad left of the family, and she was here in Norfolk, while they were hundreds of miles away up in Lancaster. But the bond between them was strong. The miles didn't matter because they were still there for each other.

Flo could hear music coming from the sitting room where everyone had gathered after the washing up and clearing away had been done, following their delicious Christmas meal. Prue was playing the piano and she recognised the introduction of *Once in Royal David's City*, and then the voices of her Rookery House family as they sang. Last year, when Thea said they were about to sing carols, Flo had volunteered to go outside to tend the animals and avoid singing them. But this year was different. Flo went into the sitting room and joined the group gathered around the piano, squeezing in to stand beside Betty and George and their mother Jess, who'd come to stay for a few days. She smiled across at Nancy, who was there with her girls, and then Flo took a deep breath and joined in.

Thea, who stood on the far side of the group, caught Flo's eye and gave her a nod, which she returned. It felt good to be singing with her friends, Flo thought. Since she arrived here, they'd become another kind of family to her, a family of friends who were just as dear to her as her blood relations.

After they'd sung a few more carols, Prue turned around on the piano stool to face them. 'Any requests?'

'Will you play *The Holly and the Ivy*?' The words tumbled out of Flo's mouth before she had time to think but instead of wishing she hadn't spoken she was glad she had. Singing her favourite carol with her Rookery House family would be the highpoint of her Christmas.

'Will you do a solo?' Hettie asked, having been at the hospital with the singing group and witnessed her performance there. 'You do it so lovely.'

'No, I want to sing it with you all, with my friends.'

Prue touched Flo's arm before turning around to face the piano and find the right page in her book of music.

This time, as Flo listened to the introductory bars, her heart kept to its normal steady rhythm. There was no sense of dread or trepidation as there had been before, just the anticipation of singing the beautiful words and notes of a song that she loved, alongside people she loved. As she began to sing, Flo realised that the shadow that had lingered over her for so long was gone. It had passed because she'd been brave enough to challenge her fears.

Lifting her chin, Flo let her voice soar with joy.

CHAPTER 24

Evie never minded being on duty on Christmas Day rather than celebrating at home. Staying in hospital during the festive season wasn't easy for their patients, so the staff always did their best to make it a special time and Evie enjoyed doing her bit. The usual jobs still had to be done, like changing dressings or taking temperatures, pulses and blood pressures, but just for today Matron Reed encouraged her nurses to turn the day into an extra-ordinary one. There'd been a Christmas meal with delicious meat from the cockerels raised on the estate and plenty of fresh vegetables from the kitchen garden. They'd even had a plum pudding and custard; the recipe had been adapted by the cook on account of rationing, but it had still tasted good.

Afterwards, the afternoon had been filled with fun and good cheer with some staff joining in parlour games with the men in the Recreation Room. Matron Reed proved to be a dab hand at playing charades. Now, a tea of sandwiches and mince pies was being served to mobile men in the Recreation Room and those bed-bound in the ward. Evie was in the Recreation

Room going around with the teapot topping up cups for the men who were there relaxing or playing games of cards while they listening to the wind-up gramophone.

'More tea, Flight Sergeant Parish?' she asked the young man who was now out of bed for a good portion of the day using a wheelchair, which enabled him to get out of the ward.

'Yes, please, Nurse Jones.' He held up his cup for her to fill.

'Have you enjoyed today?' she asked, pouring tea.

'I have. Watching Matron act out *Gone with the Wind* will live with me for quite some time!' He grinned. 'To be honest, I wasn't sure how this day would be, but it's been fun. I know it's not the same as being with your family, but I've really enjoyed myself. How about you?'

'I have enjoyed myself too. Some nurses would rather be at home but I rather like working on Christmas Day. It's not the same as a normal shift and I like that.'

'Are you up for a game of poker, Parish?' one of the other patients enquired from his place at the nearby card table.

'Count me in. Do want to play as well, Nurse Jones?' Flight Sergeant Parish asked.

'I'd better not.' She lowered her voice. 'I know Matron's in a jolly mood today but I'm not sure it would extend to me sitting around playing poker – even if it is only for matchsticks.' She gestured to the pile on the card table that they used instead of money to bet. 'Enjoy your game.'

After checking that all the men had enough tea, she left them to play and headed out into the hallway, pushing the trolley with cleared plates and the empty teapot back towards the kitchen. Stopping by the Christmas tree, she breathed in the fresh pine scent filling the air, thinking it made a lovely change from the smell of hospital disinfectant. She would miss the tree when it was taken down.

Evie heard the front door open and a gust of cold air made

the colourful baubles hanging on the tree twist and turn. She looked around to see who'd come in and was surprised to see it was Ned. He closed the door behind him and hesitated before walking towards her.

'Hello,' he said. 'Merry Christmas.'

Evie noticed his cheeks were pink from the cold outside and almost raised her hand to touch them, but reined herself in because, although she might have done that before, things were different between them now. She didn't know where she stood as she hadn't spoken to Ned since last Friday when she'd given him her answer and had only seen him from a distance at the carol concert. She was certain he'd been avoiding her. So did his sudden appearance now mean he'd come here to tell her his decision?

'Hello, Ned. Merry Christmas to you too!' Evie kept her voice calm, not wanting to give in to the emotion swirling inside her, because if this was the end, then she wanted to go out with her head held high, even if inside she was weeping. She would not show how much it hurt her. 'What brings you here on Christmas Day? It's your day off, isn't it?'

'It is. I came to find you. Can we talk for a minute or two?'

Just long enough to say his piece, Evie thought.

'I don't want anyone seeing us chatting when I should be working.' She gestured to a gap between the wall and Christmas tree where they would be hidden from the view of anyone coming into the hall from the wards or Recreation Room. 'Let's talk over there,' she said, leading him and then turning to face him. 'What do you want to talk about?'

'Us, of course!' Ned ran a hand through his dark brown hair. 'I've been thinking about what you said last week and...'

'It's all right. I understand,' Evie interrupted. 'I won't make it awkward for you. I'll look for another job and move away.'

'What?' Ned frowned. 'No! I don't want you to do that.' He

took hold of her hand in his. 'I couldn't bear not to be with you, Evie. I love you and if you feel you can't…' he lowered his voice, so it couldn't be heard by anyone other than her above the tinny sound of the gramophone music spilling out into the hall from the Recreation Room. 'If you can't marry again, then I respect that. After what you went through before, I understand your reasoning. I wish it was different, but it is as it is. Being with you is the most important thing in my life. It's what I want more than anything.'

'More than getting married?' Evie whispered.

'Yes, more than getting married. Thea was right, I see that now. Marriage is just a legal formality. It certainly doesn't guarantee happiness – there are plenty of examples where it has brought the opposite for a husband or a wife, or both. I want us to be together because we *want* to be. Let's do as you suggest.' His eyes were full of hope and love behind his glasses. 'Please say yes.'

Evie didn't need to think about her answer. 'Yes! Let's do it as soon as we can.' She flung her arms around him and hugged him. 'I thought you were going to say no, that you couldn't agree.'

He released her but still held on to her upper arms, his eyes looking into hers. 'I want you to be happy. That's the most important thing, and we will live in every way as husband and wife, loving and caring for each other. Nothing else matters.'

He kissed her and Evie felt all her worries of the past weeks melting away. She could look forward to a future here with Ned beside her. And she felt safe, because Ned was the right man for her.

'If you're going to be kissing behind the Christmas tree,' a familiar soft Scottish voice called out from above, causing them to spring apart, 'then at least make use of the mistletoe!'

Evie looked up in horror to see Matron Reed peering

down over the banister at them from the top of the stairs. The older woman pointed to the bunch of mistletoe hanging from the middle of the ceiling in the hallway. The way Matron's cheeks were unusually rosy and the fact that she hadn't torn Evie off a strip for kissing Ned while on duty suggested that Matron may have been having a celebratory sherry or two with her mince pies.

Sensing Ned hesitate, Evie said, 'Come on, I think we'd best do as Matron asks.' She held up her hand for Ned to take, and he led her out into the middle of the hall.

Evie looked up at the bunch of mistletoe which had been ordered along with the other greenery to decorate the hall. She wondered if this hadn't been in Matron's mind all along, after she was put in charge of decorations. She thought it probably was, and squeezing Ned's hand, she laughed.

'What are you waiting for, Mr Blythe?' Matron's voice called out as she descended the stairs. 'I might turn a blind eye for a minute or two, but remember, Nurse Jones is on duty. So if you're going to kiss her under the mistletoe, you'd best get on with it.' She glanced at the watch on the front of her uniform as she swept by them, heading towards the Recreation Room and calling over her shoulder. 'Two minutes, Nurse Jones, then that trolley needs to go to the kitchen.'

'You heard Matron,' Evie said with a mischievous grin. 'I...' but her words were silenced as Ned kissed her.

This was a Christmas that she would remember for the rest of her life, Evie thought as she kissed him back, her heart filling with happiness for what they had now and for their wonderful future together.

Dear Reader,

I hope you enjoyed reading *Christmas Carols at Rookery House* and catching up with Flo and Evie again in this festive story.

Prue, Thea and Hettie and the other residents of Great Plumstead will return next in *New Beginnings at Rookery House*.

I love hearing from readers – so please do get in touch via:

Facebook: be friends on **Rosie Hendry Books,** or join my
private readers group - **Rosie Hendry's Reader Group**
X (Twitter): @hendry_rosie
Instagram: rosiehendryauthor
Website: **www.rosiehendry.com**

On my website, you can sign up to get my newsletter delivered straight to your inbox, with all the latest on my writing life, exclusive looks behind the scenes of my work, and reader competitions.

If you have the time and would like to share your thoughts about this book, do please leave a review. I read and appreciate each one as it's wonderful to hear what you think. Reviews also encourage other readers to try my books.

With warmest wishes,

Rosie

IF YOU ENJOYED CHRISTMAS CAROLS AT ROOKERY
HOUSE...

It would be wonderful if you could spare a few minutes to leave a star rating, or write a review, at the retailer where you bought this book.

Reviews don't need to be long – a sentence or two is absolutely fine. They make a huge difference to authors, helping us know what readers think of our books and what they particularly enjoy. Reviews also help other readers discover new books to try for themselves.

You might also tell family and friends you think would enjoy this book.

Thank you!

HEAR MORE FROM ROSIE

Want to keep up to date with Rosie's latest releases?

Subscribe to her newsletter on her website.
www.rosiehendry.com

Subscribers get Rosie's newsletter delivered to their inbox and are always the first to know about the latest books, as well as getting exclusive behind the scenes news, plus reader competitions.

You can unsubscribe at any time and your email will never be shared with anyone else.

ACKNOWLEDGMENTS

A huge thank you to all my readers who have taken the Rookery House books and characters to their hearts.

Thanks to the fantastic team who help me create the books — editor, Catriona Robb and cover designer, Andrew Brown. Also to my author friends and especially those of the Famous Five whose friendship, chats and laughs together are such a joy.

Finally, thank you to David, who supports me in all I do.

Have you met the East End Angels?

Winnie, Frankie and Bella are brave ambulance crew who rescue casualties of the London Blitz.

BOOK 1 - USA and Canada edition

BOOK 1 - UK and rest world English edition

Available in ebook, paperback and audiobook.

ALSO BY ROSIE HENDRY

East End Angels series

East End Angels

Secrets of the East End Angels

Christmas with the East End Angels

Victory for the East End Angels

East End Angels Together Again

Rookery House series

The Mother's Day Club

The Mother's Day Victory

A Wartime Welcome at Rookery House

A Wartime Christmas at Rookery House

Digging for Victory at Rookery House

A Christmas Baby at Rookery House

Home Comforts at Rookery House

Christmas Carols at Rookery House

Standalone

Secrets and Promises

A Home from Home

Love on a Scottish Island

A Pocketful of Stories

Rosie Hendry lived and worked in the USA before settling back in her home county of Norfolk, England, where she lives in a village by the sea with her family. She likes walking in nature, reading and growing all sorts of produce and flowers in her garden — especially roses.

Rosie writes stories from the heart that are inspired by historical records, where gems of social history are often to be found. Her interest in the WWII era was sparked by her father's many tales of growing up at that time.

Rosie is the winner of the 2022 Romantic Novelists' Association (RNA) award for historical romantic sagas, with *The Mother's Day Club*, the first of her series set during wartime at Rookery House. Her novels set in the London Blitz, the *East End Angels* series, have been described as 'Historical fiction at its very best!'.

To find out more visit **www.rosiehendry.com**

Made in the USA
Columbia, SC
22 October 2024

44857796R00079